W9-AND-348

WEREWOLVES

WEREWOLVES

Zachary Graves

CHARTWELL
BOOKS, INC.

CONTENTS

INTRODUCTION

The werewolf is a dark and mysterious creature. Folklore from all over the globe tells stories of massive wolves stalking the countryside for prey, terrorizing and mutilating victims. These stories have given much to popular fiction writers, who have built on the legend, adding rules and dimensions to this ancient beast. In medieval folklore, there are numerous tales of remote villages being torn apart by werewolves with an uncontrollable bloodlust and an insatiable appetite for human flesh. By day, however, these creatures are nowhere to be seen. The only evidence of their existence being the discovery of dead bodies apparently torn apart by something with claws, and bloody paw prints marking the perpetrator's last movements.

Craving for Human Meat

Often, the man behind the werewolf committed such heinous acts of violence that were so sickening to society, that he was deemed to be working for the devil himself. A cannibal killer displays the same cravings for human meat and blood as the midnight predator, the werewolf. It is not surprising that murderers got dubbed werewolves, and were usually executed in a truly torturous way. Some people, however, did believe absolutely in the werewolf legend. Wolves were hunted and slaughtered as a result, for fear that they may metamorphose into a much more dangerous beast at night.

By day, detecting a potential werewolf was a matter of looking for clues. People with eyebrows that met over the bridge of their nose were often suspected, as were those with hair inside their legs, an affliction difficult to prove until the suspect was dead, sadly. Through the werewolf panic that took place in medieval Europe, people learnt to avoid areas where the beasts were believed to congregate. Precautions were taken against becoming a werewolf oneself; people were told not to drink from 'enchanted' streams or accept unusual ointments or salves from strangers. The seventh child born into a family would often be killed at birth or given away, in the belief that one day it would be answering the call of the wild. Donning a belt made of wolfskin was believed to transform you instantly into a werewolf, as was wearing a lycanthropic flower or eating the flesh of a werewolf's victim. There was a lot to remember in these deeply superstitious and suspicious times.

Man's Alter Ego

As time passed and advances in psychology and medicine were made, mental illness soon was blamed for man's alter ego bursting out uninvited. A werewolf is, of course, a perfect metaphor for the 'duality of man'. There is a raw, wild power within each of us and when we are crossed, we feel a strong urge to retaliate. The rage can escalate until we can contain it no longer. For most of us, we can tame this inner beast through rational

Movie Portrait from *Werewolf of London*, Stuart Walker 1935.

thought. But for some, it is impossible to suppress and when the monster inside takes control, the results can be devastating. Andrei Chikatilo, the notorious Russian serial killer, was so consumed by his bestial urges that he literally consumed parts of his victims. Someone who acts this way is alien to most of society, and it is easy to see why such animalistic behaviour was attributed to supernatural forces in times past. Perhaps this was easier than admitting that humans have the ability to tear each other open and feast on the exposed body parts.

Werewolf fiction finds its foundation in folklore, and the werewolf is part of the horror pantheon which grows ever more popular. The werewolf is the savage creature alongside the recently romanticized vampire and the slightly comedic zombie. The werewolf has a pulse, giving it an immediate advantage over its supernatural colleagues, and also has the benefit of being able to enjoy the daytime, something the others have to miss out on - unless you're the rather sparkly Edward Cullen, that is. Red blood runs through a werewolf's veins along with primal instincts that make them more than a match for the vampire or zombie.

Thanks to folklore inspiring popular fiction, the werewolf myth has been presented to us in literature, film, television and music. Scottish author Robert Louis Stevenson wrote *The Strange Case of Dr Jekyll and Mr Hyde* in 1886. It is a portrait of a man with

Scene still from *Ginger Snaps*, John Fawcett, 2000.

a divided self, a double consciousness - an allegory for the good and evil within everyone. Jekyll describes his evil double Mr Hyde as 'the animal within me' and a 'caged creature that cannot be denied'. This may not be a werewolf story, but it remains the archetype for all the werewolf and transformation stories that followed. In the same way that *Frankenstein* spawned the re-animated zombie and *Dracula* gave life to the vampire, *Jekyll and Hyde* taught us about the 'wolf within' exposed by drinking a potion of drugs. Other means of transforming in werewolf fiction can be through a magical amulet, a curse or hex, or simply through bad genes. Scott Howard, in *Teen Wolf*, becomes a werewolf as puberty kicks in, a concept also used in *Ginger Snaps*, albeit tackled completely differently. One of the most famous werewolf movies, 1941's *The Wolf Man*, introduced us to Larry Talbot (played by Lon Chaney Jnr) and many of the werewolf rules with which we are are now so familiar. It taught us that transformation from man to werewolf takes place under the glare of the full moon and that silver (a bullet or simply an object) is the most effective weapon against the wolfman.

Remorse and Regret

The human form of a werewolf, in fiction, is often a decent character during daytime. After a savage night out, the werewolf will wake in human form, full of remorse. The werewolves of *Being Human* and *Buffy the Vampire Slayer*, are so concerned for their condition that they lock themselves up when they know the transformation is coming. Remus Lupin, in *Harry Potter and the Prisoner of Azkaban*, is so disturbed by his affliction that he takes a daily Wolfsbane potion to control his inner beast. The werewolves of

Stephenie Meyer's *Twilight* series have a more protective nature, and 'phase' when they need to protect others or defend themselves. The representation of Jacob Black in his werewolf state is much more cuddly than the werewolves of *Dog Soldiers*. The werewolf is constantly battling with the two sides of his character. By day, the human-wolf is deeply ashamed of its deadly night-time excursions, but under darkness their werewolf conscience is clear and they have no qualms about ripping innocent flesh.

The 16th-century physician, botanist, alchemist, astrologer, and occultist, Paracelsus, believed that a person has two spirits - an animal spirit and a human spirit. The more dominant side of a person's earthly character forms their spirit in the afterlife. Carnal and bestial human cravings on earth doom the phantom of the afterlife to roam eternity in the shape of a wild animal such as a wolf, wreaking havoc and retribution on earthly beings.

Silver Bullets

It is no wonder that our imagination and culture is so filled with lupine imagery and legend. Recent studies have shown just how ordered and hierarchical the wolf's society is. Man and wolves have a lot in common. Man lives in a kind of pack - the family - like the wolf, and is also one of the great survivors in the story of evolution. Indeed, the wolf can be said to have been a rival to mankind in the struggle for dominance. Through the ages, we have fought for the same food, especially when it was in short supply. It was kill or be killed. A man, unarmed, is no match for the wolf, but man invented weapons. Once, of course, it was spears and bows; now it is guns. Remember to load those silver bullets though - just to be sure.

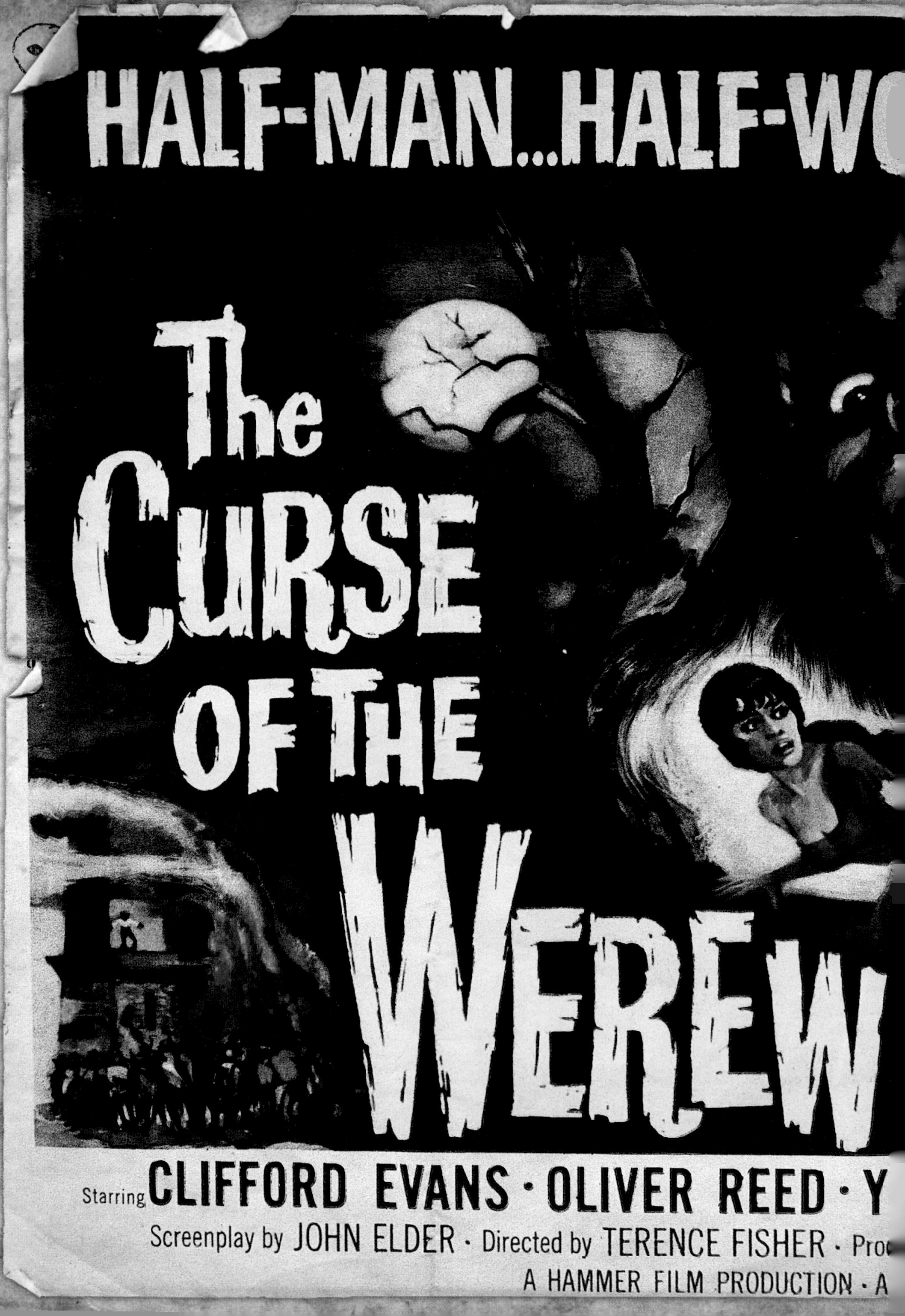
HALF-MAN...HALF-WO
The CURSE OF THE WEREW
Starring CLIFFORD EVANS · OLIVER REED · Y
Screenplay by JOHN ELDER · Directed by TERENCE FISHER · Proc
A HAMMER FILM PRODUCTION · A

Film poster for *The Curse of the Werewolf*, Terence Fisher, 1961

MY
Y
of
WERE

TH the WOLF

Generally speaking, in myth and folklore, a werewolf is a human who has the ability to transform itself - shapeshift - into an anthropomorphic wolf-like creature. It achieves this state in a variety of ways and the transformation, as noted by Petronius in his writing and by numerous other writers, is often associated with the appearance of the full moon.

SUPERHUMAN STRENGTH

Werewolves are often described as possessing superhuman strength and enhanced senses that are more powerful than mere wolves and certainly greater than those of humans. It possesses all the attributes of a wolf - powerful jaws lined with sharp teeth and large paws that are capable of doing a great deal of damage to another creature. However, in some stories, werewolves are also said to have killed with daggers or knives.

In their human, unaltered form, werewolves are reputed to display obvious signs of their alternative form. The eyebrows, for instance, of a human who transforms into a werewolf, are often said to meet at the bridge of the nose. They have curved fingernails, ears set low on the side of the head and they walk with a loping, swinging stride. They are reputed to be listless, lacking in energy and anxious to avoid direct sunlight. They also find cooked meat repellent. It is often said that the only part of the body that does not change when a human transforms into a werewolf are the eyes. They remain human - although they may, when the creature is enraged, appear to be on fire. They are also unable to shed any tears; werewolves, unsurprisingly, cannot cry.

It is said that if you cut the flesh of a werewolf in human form, beneath the flesh you will see its fur. The Russians, meanwhile, maintain that someone can be proved to be a werewolf by the bristles under his tongue. The appearance of werewolves varies from culture to culture, but they are generally shown as not possessing a tail, much like their supernatural counterparts; witches, who never have tails when they take on the form of an animal.

In the part of Scandinavia known as Fennoscandia, werewolves were traditionally old women with claws that were coated in poison. They had the power of being able to paralyze cattle and children with their gaze. Meanwhile, in Serbia, *vulkodlaks* (used in Serbian folklore for both werewolves and vampires) were believed to gather together during winter. They would strip off their wolfskins and hang them from trees. Whenever they gathered together, they would take one wolfskin and throw it on the fire, thereby releasing its possessor from the curse that had transformed it into a vampire or werewolf.

In Haiti, there are werewolf-like creatures known as *jé-rouges* who try to steal children from their mothers in the night, waking them and while they are still in a drowsy state, asking them for permission to take their child. Disorientated mothers sometimes say yes and live to regret that one word for the remainder of their lives.

FROM WEREWOLF TO HUMAN

The return to human form is a devastating experience for the werewolf. He is often shown at this stage to be fragile and weak and is likely to be severely depressed. The magnitude of the crimes committed while in animal form renders the werewolf remorseful, suffering from melancholia and terrible pangs of guilt. Amongst the terrible crimes committed in medieval Europe was the werewolf's horrific habit of eating recently buried corpses.

Cynocephali effigies, woodcut of man with wolf head, Aldrovandi 1642, Europe.

BECOMING A WEREWOLF

Legend and folklore describe a wide variety of ways to become a werewolf. The simplest of all, and possibly the most common in historical legend, is to remove all clothing and don a belt made of wolfskin or, sometimes, human skin removed from the body of an executed criminal. The belt, or girdle, as it is sometimes called, should be three fingers wide.

Of course, movie depictions demonstrate that another common way to acquire the power of being transformed from man to wolf is to be bitten by a werewolf, the creature's saliva entering its victim's bloodstream and creating the power. This, however, is scorned by some who would say that if someone is bitten by a werewolf, he or she very rarely survives the encounter and would not, therefore, be alive to become a werewolf.

FULL MOON

In Italy, France and Germany, it was said that a man could turn into a werewolf if he slept outside on a certain Wednesday or Friday night in summer, with the full moon shining directly on his face.

Drinking water from the tracks of wolves is recommended if you have the desire to become a werewolf, or even drinking from certain streams which are either enchanted

or where wolves drink. Eating the flesh - in particular the heart - of a wolf or something killed by a wolf is said to be another way to become a werewolf. In fact, Egbert, Archbishop of York, who died in 766, proclaimed that the flesh of animals that had been attacked and killed by wolves should not be eaten as a precaution against the people who consumed it becoming werewolves.

However, some sources also say that eating the flesh of a wolf or its victim has the opposite effect, that it actually strengthens the person who consumes the wolf's or its victim's flesh against a range of magical enchantments. Eating human flesh is also a means of becoming a werewolf, especially the flesh of violent criminals.

ENCHANTED WATERS

Elliot O'Donnell, in his classic book on the subject, *Werewolves*, goes into some detail as to how to become a werewolf in Sweden or Norway.

He writes that the supplicant should find a lycanthropous stream. Lycanthropous water differs subtly from ordinary water and it takes a trained eye to spot it. It emits a faint odour unlike any other and it has a 'lurid sparkle' to it that seems to suggest some internal life. As it flows, the sound it makes is reminiscent of the sound - or, at least, mutterings and whispers - of human voices. At night, terrifying screams and groans come from it and animals avoid it and if brought close to it, cower and howl in fear.

Kneeling by the side of the stream, the person should chant the following:

Tis night! 'tis night! and the moon shines white
Over pine and snow-capped hill;
The shadows stray through burn and brae
And dance in the sparkling rill.
Tis night! 'tis night! and the devil's light
Casts glimmering beams around.
The maras dance, the nisses prance
On the flower-enamelled ground.
Tis night! 'tis night! and the werwolf's might
Makes man and nature shiver.
Yet its fierce grey head and stealthy tread
Are nought to thee, oh river!
River, river, river.
Oh water strong, that swirls along,
I prithee a werwolf make me.
Of all things dear, my soul, I swear,
In death shall not forsake thee.

He should then strike the banks of the stream three times with his forehead and dip his head into the river three times, each time swallowing a mouthful of the enchanted water. With that, he or she has become a werewolf internally and 24 hours later, the first metamorphosis will begin.

LYCANTHROPOUS FLOWERS

To become a werewolf, Swedish and Norwegian supplicants might also pluck a lycanthropous flower and wear it after sunset on a night when the moon is full. Lycanthropous flowers, like lycanthropous water, possess qualities that are peculiar to them. Their scent is said to be reminiscent of death and their sap is white and sticky,

although they look much the same as other flowers, normally white or yellow.

The lycanthropous flower crops up in a number of different cultures. There is a story told about the Kloska family who lived in the village of Kerovitch on the Romanian side of the Transylvanian Alps. Ivan and Olga Kloska were the children of a shopkeeper. One morning, out with their mother who was washing clothes in a stream behind their house, the two children wandered off. They started to pick flowers but suddenly Ivan heard a scream. Turning round, he discovered that his sister had fallen into a pit that had been covered up by weeds and brambles. He climbed down to make sure she was not hurt. She was fine, but pointed

out to him a strange flower growing down there. It was a vivid white flower, a little like a sunflower but soft and pulpy and emitting a sweet, sickly smell. Olga said she was going to wear it, but Ivan was worried because it looked more like a fungus than a flower and warned her against it. When she began to cry, however, he gave in and allowed her to fix it to her dress. When she asked him if it looked nice, however, he suddenly became frightened when he looked at her face which was changing into the face of something else - a wolf!

A Deadly Flower

Ivan tried to clamber out of the pit to alert his mother, but a struggle ensued. Their mother, hearing the commotion, ran to the spot to find Ivan kneeling on the ground attempting to keep at bay a grey wolf that had already bitten him and was now trying to get close enough to sink its yellow fangs into his throat. He shouted to his mother that the wolf was Olga, explaining about the flower as the wolf lunged at him. The children's mother had with her a skewer that she used to fix her washing line to a tree, but she also had a dilemma. If she killed the wolf she would lose her daughter; if she did not, she would lose her son. She made her decision and plunged the skewer into the wolf's eye. An hour later, a villager on his way home, heard strange sounds of laughter. He went to the side of the pit and leaned over. 'Vera Kloska! What have you there?', he screamed. 'Ha! ha! ha!' came the answer. 'My children! Don't they look funny? Olga has such a pretty white flower in her buttonhole, and Ivan a red stain on his forehead. They are deaf - they won't reply when I speak to them. See if you can make them hear.' The villager shook his head. 'They'll never hear

Attracting a Werewolf

Certain flowers, such as lily of the valley, marigolds and azaleas are said to attract werewolves, and diamonds are thought to have the same power. In southern France, and in other places, the full moon is the time when a *loup-garou* is transformed from a human to wolf, whether it is done voluntarily or not. Often the way they make the transformation is by diving into a pool or a fountain from which they emerge covered in hair and savage in manner. To return to their human form, they jump back into the same water.

Anglo-Dutch antiquarian, Richard Verstegan, wrote in *Restitution of Decayed Intelligence* in 1628:

The werewolves are certayne sorcerers, who having anointed their bodies with an ointment which they make by the instinct of the devil, and putting on a certayne inchaunted girdle, doe not onely unto the view of others seeme as wolves, but to their owne thinking have both the shape and nature of wolves, so long as they weare the said girdle. And they do dispose themselves as very wolves, in wourrying and killing, and most of humane creatures.

again in this world, poor mad woman,' he went on. 'You've murdered them.'

OLD RUSSIAN SPELL FOR BECOMING A WEREWOLF

To become a werewolf, go into a forest and find a tree that has been cut down. Stick a small copper knife into it and walk in a circle around the tree reciting the following:

In the wide, sweeping ocean, on the island Bujan

On the open plain the Moon shines on an aspen stump

Into the green wood, into the gloomy vale

Towards the herd creeps a shaggy wolf

His fangs sharpened for the horned cattle

But into the wood the wolf does not go

He dives not into the shadowy vale

Moon, moon! Golden horned moon!

Melt the bullet; blunt the hunter's knife

Splinter the shepherd's staff

Cast terror upon all cattle

Upon men and all creeping things

That they may not seize the grey wolf

That they may not rend his warm hide!

My word is binding, firmer than sleep

More binding than the promise of heroes!

Afterwards, jump over the tree three times and you will have become a werewolf.

According to Elliott O'Donnell there are a number of ways to become a werewolf. In some cases, it is hereditary, it runs in the family and there is nothing they can do about it, if the gene is passed on to them. In other cases, it is acquired through black magic ritual in rites that vary according to

locality. One thing is for certain, however, according to O'Donnell, anyone who wants to become a werewolf must believe one hundred percent in the supernatural entities that provide such powers.

The person wishing to transform into a werewolf must find an isolated spot, far from other people. The preferred locations would be deserts, remote forests or mountain-tops.

THE WITCHING HOUR

Timing is, of course, critical. It goes without saying that a night must be chosen when the moon is new or strong, because at that time, the planetary influences are at their most favourable. A perfectly flat piece of ground should be chosen and at midnight, a circle of no less than seven feet in radius should be marked, with chalk, and if that is not possible, with string. Inside this, from the same centre point, should be marked a smaller circle, three feet in radius. In the centre of these circles, a fire should be lit and over the fire should be set up an iron tripod from which should hang an iron container of water. When the water begins to boil, handfuls of any three of the following should be tossed - asafoetida (a plant also known as devil's dung), parsley, opium, hemlock, henbane, saffron, aloe, poppyseed or solanum. As they are thrown into the container, the following should be chanted:

Spirits from the deep
Who never sleep,
Be kind to me.

Spirits from the grave
Without a soul to save
Be kind to me.

> Spirits of the trees
> That grow upon the leas,
> Be kind to me
>
> Spirits of the air
> Foul and black, not fair,
> Be kind to me.
>
> Water spirits hateful,
> To ships and bathers fateful,
> Be kind to me.
>
> Spirits of earthbound dead,
> That glide with noiseless tread,
> Be kind to me.
>
> Spirits of heat and fire,
> Destructive in your ire,
> Be kind to me.
>
> Spirits of cold and ice,
> Patrons of crime and vice,
> Be kind to me.
>
> Wolves, vampires, satyrs, ghost!
> Elect of all the devilish hosts!
> I pray you send hither,
> Send hither, send hither,
> The great grey shape that makes men shiver!
>
> Shiver, shiver, shiver!
> Come! Come! Come!

The person seeking to achieve these special powers should then remove his clothing and smear his body with the fat of a recently killed animal (a cat is best) which should have aniseed, camphor and opium added to it. Around the loins, a girdle or belt made of the skin of a wolf should be tied. The supplicant should then kneel inside the circumference of the first circle and await the arrival of 'the Unknown'. It will be clear that the Unknown is about to appear when the fire burns blue.

The Arrival of the Spirit

The great spirit may arrive in a variety of ways. There may be an unusually profound silence just before but there may also be a great deal of noise - bangs, crashes, groans and screams. He may not become visible, but his presence will be felt through an abnormal chill in the air and the supplicant will be filled with terror. He may appear in the form of a huntsman - his most common form - or in the form of a monster, part man, part beast. Occasionally, he may appear hazy and will only partially materialize.

O'Donnell declares this force not to be the devil, but certainly a malevolent, supernatural power that he claims probably participated in the creation of the Earth and the other planets. There are other methods you could follow to become a werewolf without undergoing such a terrifying experience. O'Donnell suggests eating the brains of a wolf, or drinking water taken from the footprint of a wolf or even by drinking water from a stream from which three or more wolves have been seen to drink.

THE EIGI EINHAMMR

In Norway and Iceland, there were men who were described as *eigi einhammr* - 'not of one skin'. They were supposed to be able to assume other bodies as well as the natures of the creatures whose bodies they took. By this transformation, the *eigi einhammr* acquired extraordinary powers; his strength was multiplied several times over because he retained his own but added to it the strength of the creature whose form he had taken. A man thus transmogrified was known as a *hamrammr*.

There were various ways to effect the necessary change. Sometimes, a pelt was thrown over the body and in this case the transformation was instant. On other oc-

casions, however, the soul deserted the human body and entered the body of the creature being subsumed. The human body was left in a cataleptic state, seeming dead to the uninitiated. Another way to effect the change was by incantation. This method left the human form unaltered but the eyes of onlookers were charmed so that they could see him only in his selected, altered form.

The *eigi einhammr*, in his bestial form, is recognizable only by his eyes. They can never be altered. His behaviour, however, will always be that of the creature whose shape he has assumed, although his human intelligence and wit will remain with him. Therefore, he can do what the animal will do, whilst retaining the ability to do what a man can do.

THE POWER OF WOLFSKIN

There is a story in the 13th century *Saga of the Völsungs* that includes the wolfskin method for becoming a werewolf. Two young men, Sigmund and Sinfjötli, were wandering through a wood one day when they came upon a large house. Inside there were two men in the midst of a deep sleep. A magic spell had been cast on them, condemning them to be wolves for nine days. On the tenth day they were permitted to remove the enchanted wolfskins that made them werewolves and become men again.

From Men to Werewolves

The two young men decided to steal the wolfskins while the men slept. They sneaked in, grabbed them and ran away. Once they were far from the cottage they put the skins on and were immediately transformed into wolves. They both howled and realized they could understand wolf language. They made a pact to go their separate ways, but agreed that if one of them found himself being hunted by more than seven men, he would howl and the other would rush to his aid. A few days later, Sigmund encountered a group of hunters who tried to kill him. He howled and Sinfjötli arrived and killed all the humans. Some time after that, Sinfjötli was attacked by eleven hunters, but he succeeded in killing all of them. Sigmund arrived on the scene by accident and asked his friend why he did not summon him; there were more than seven hunters, after all. Sinfjötli was arrogant, however, and told Sigmund he did not need his help in dealing with so few men.

Changing Back

Sigmund was offended by what he took as an insult to his prowess. He became enraged and launched himself at Sinfjötli, biting him in the throat. As he stepped away, his friend lay on the ground, not moving. Sigmund was instantly ashamed of what he had done, both putting on the wolfskin and attacking Sinfjötli. He picked up his friend and carried him back to the house in the woods, now vacated by the two men. As he approached the house, however, he caught sight of two weasels fighting. One bit the other's throat and immediately ran into a thicket to return with a leaf that it put against the wound of the other. Instantly, the injured weasel was healed and seemed almost as if he had never been hurt. Sigmund went out in search of such a leaf, when suddenly a raven appeared, carrying a leaf in its beak. Sigmund placed it against his friend's wound and Sinfjötli was healed. On the tenth day of their adventure, they resumed their human forms, took the wolfskins off and placed them on a fire where they were reduced to ashes.

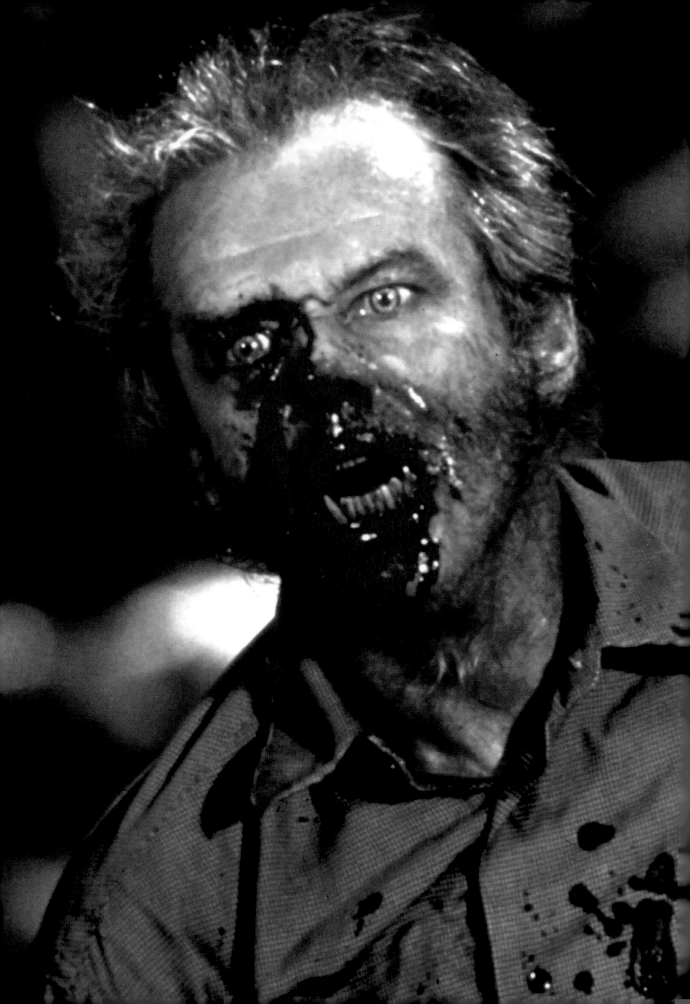

Scene still showing Jack Nicholson as Will Randall in *Wolf*, Mike Nichols, 1994.

TRANSFORMATION & METAMORPHOSIS

There is a great deal of inconsistency in the various descriptions of the metamorphosis from man to wolf, and in the creature that results from it. Sometimes this change is brought about at will and on other occasions it is governed by the time of day or by the seasons. Sometimes the beast is half-man, half-wolf, a creature that walks on its hind legs; on other occasions it is a wolf, to all intents and purposes. Even when it is killed, there is inconsistency. Sometimes, it retains the shape of the wolf; at others, it transforms back to its original human form.

Even in its behaviour as humans, there is a degree of disagreement. Werewolves that are unwillingly made thus by outside agencies need not be savage and cruel in human form. In many tales, they are good, kind and gentle people until they are changed into wolves. In some cases of involuntary metamorphosis and most of voluntary, the werewolf is an evil person to begin with and, in his wolf form, this creature is a blend of beast and man, with all his subtle ingenuity and powers of reasoning.

CANNIBALISTIC TENDENCIES

People in search of a rational explanation, suggest that belief in werewolves is traceable to the craving for blood which some people possess and which is sometimes accompanied by hallucinations that make the subject believe that he is a werewolf. They speak of tribes of cannibals in Africa who use their neighbours' fear of wolves to satisfy their need for human flesh, by dressing themselves in wolfskins and pouncing on their enemies at night, thus creating rumours that the half-eaten remains that are discovered are the work of half-human, half-wolf creatures that roam isolated places after dark. Thus does the existence of such creatures, through time, become an established fact.

THE PROCESS OF METAMORPHOSIS

German reformer, physician and scholar, Caspar Peucer, wrote in his *Commentarius De Praecipiuys Diuinationum Genribus* in 1553:

As for me I had formerly regarded as ridiculous and fabulous the stories I had heard concerning the transformation of men into wolves; but I have learnt from reliable sources, and from the testimony of reliable witnesses, that such things are not

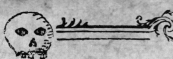
at all doubtful or incredible, since they tell of such transformations taking place twelve days after Christmas in Livonia and the adjacent countries; as they have been proved to be true by the confessions of those who have been imprisoned and tortured for such crimes. Here is the manner in which it is done.

Immediately after Christmas day is past, a lame boy goes around calling these slaves of the devil, of which there are a great number, and enjoining them to follow him. If they procrastinate or go too slowly, there immediately appears a tall man with a whip whose thongs are made of iron chains, with which he urges them onwards, and sometimes lashes the poor wretches so cruelly, that the marks of the whips remain on their bodies till long afterwards, and cause them the greatest pain. As soon as they have set out on the road, they are all changed into wolves.

...They travel in thousands, having for their conductor the bearer of the whip, after whom they march. When they reach the fields, they rush upon the cattle they find there, tearing and carrying away all they can, and doing much other damage; but they are not permitted to touch or wound persons. When they approach any rivers, their guide separates the waters with his whip so they seem to open up and leave a dry space by which to cross.

At the end of twelve days the whole band scatters, and everyone returns to his home, having regained his own proper form. This transformation, they say, comes about in this wise. Those who are changed fall suddenly to the ground as if seized with epilepsy, and there they lie without life or motion. Their actual bodies do not move from the spot where they have fallen, nor do their limbs turn to the hairy limbs of a wolf, but the soul or spirit by some fascination quits the inert body and enters the *spectrum* of a wolf, and when they have glutted their foul lupine lusts and cravings, by the Devil's power, the

soul re-enters the former human body, whose members are then energized by the return of life.

In many accounts, the transition is extremely painful and is associated with the appearance of the full moon, as noted by the medieval chronicler Gervase of Tilbury. This notion, however, was rarely associated with the werewolf until the idea was picked up by modern fiction writers, presumably because of the dramatic effect it gave a transition, as if a man transforming into a wolf was not dramatic enough.

"He soon emerged in the form of a Wolf"
THE WERE-WOLVES.

CURSE OF THE WEREWOLF

There are many reasons one may become a werewolf, and committing crimes against the Church and being excommunicated is one of them. The story is told of Hugues III of Campdavaine, the Count of Saint-Pol in the area of the Somme in northern France who destroyed the Abbey of Saint-Riquier, killing the clergy inside as well as many people who were taking refuge within its walls. He agreed with Pope Innocent III that he would assuage his sin by constructing three new abbeys, but it seems as if that was not sufficient penance. After he died in 1141, his ghost was often seen, in the shape of a black wolf, rattling heavy metal chains that weighed him down, howling as he roamed through the abbey of Saint-Riquier.

King John of England was another example, excommunicated by the same pope, Innocent III; his ghost was also seen in lupine form long after he died. In France it was thought that the *loup-garou* was sometimes a metamorphosis forced upon the body of a damned person, who, after having been tormented in his grave, had torn his way out of it. The first stage in the process consisted of devouring the cerecloth which enveloped his face and then as his moans and muffled howls emanated from the tomb, through the gloom of night, the earth of the grave began to heave, and at last, with a scream, surrounded by an otherworldly glare, and exhaling a fetid odour, he burst out of the earth as a wolf.

THE CURSE OF SEVEN

In East Friesland, it is believed, that when seven girls succeed each other in one family, that one of them would certainly be a werewolf. Needless to say, young men are slightly reluctant to court one of seven sisters. It was also said that the seventh son of a seventh son became a werewolf and this is the belief in Galician, Portuguese and Brazilian folklore. This belief was also promulgated in northern Argentina where the werewolf is known as a *lobizon*. For fear of having a werewolf in the family, a seventh son of a seventh son was customarily abandoned after birth, killed or given away to people who knew nothing of the child's history.

Scene Still from *The Wolfman*, Joe Johnston, 2009.

INVOLUNTARY WEREWOLVES

Evil people such as sorcerers and witches can become werewolves voluntarily in order to commit violent crimes, while they may also create involuntary werewolves by casting spells on innocent people. People can also become involuntary werewolves by being born at the wrong time, such as under a full moon or as a result of suffering from an illness such as epilepsy. In Campania in Italy, it is believed that anyone born on Christmas night was liable to be a werewolf for their entire life, while in Sicily that fate was ascribed to anyone born under a new moon.

SILVER BULLETS & WOLFSBANE

One of the few ways to stop someone being a werewolf, was simply to kill him and, according to some sources, that could only be achieved with the use of a silver bullet. Other effective, but sometimes bizarre, methods include: removal of the wolfskin belt or girdle, chopping off a limb which forces the creature to revert to human form, kneeling in one spot for a hundred years, being reproached for being a werewolf, being saluted with the sign of the cross, being addressed three times by your baptismal name, being struck three times on the forehead with a knife or having at least three drops of blood drawn from the body of the afflicted person.

Some folk tales speak of throwing an iron object at the werewolf to force him to revert to his human form. As with a vampire, driving a stake through the heart of a werewolf will bring an end to its activities. A sword blessed on the altar of a chapel dedicated to Saint Hubert may also be used to kill a werewolf. However, the only certain way to destroy a werewolf and ensure that it does not succeed in reviving or becoming a vampire is to cremate its head, its heart or its entire body.

ST THOMAS AQUINAS

The power of transforming others into wild beasts was ascribed not only to wicked sorcerers, witches and the devil, but to Christian saints. As philosopher and theologian, St Thomas Aquinas wrote, 'All angels, good and bad have the power of transmuting our bodies.' This story is told of St Patrick, for instance in the centuries-old Norse text, the *Konungs Skuggsjá*:

There is still another wonder in that country which must seem quite incredible; nevertheless, those who dwell in the land affirm the truth of it and ascribe it to the anger of a holy man. It is told that when the holy Patricus preached Christianity in that country, there was one clan which opposed him more stubbornly than any other clan in the land; and those people strove to do insult in many ways both to God and to the holy man. And when he was preaching the faith to them as to others and came to confer with them where they held their assemblies they adopted the plan of howling at them like wolves.

When he saw that he could do very little to promote his mission among these people, he grew very wroth and prayed

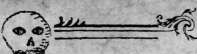

God to send some affliction upon them to be shared by their posterity as a constant reminder of their disobedience. Later these clansmen did suffer a fitting and severe though very marvelous punishment, for it is told that all the members of that clan are changed into wolves for a period and roam through the woods feeding upon the same food as wolves; but they are worse than wolves, for in all their wiles they have the wit of men, though they are as eager to devour men as to destroy other creatures. It is reported that this affliction comes every seventh winter, while in the intervening years they are men; others suffer it continuously for seven winters and are never struck again.

According to legend, St Patrick also punished the Welsh king Vereticus by turning him and his followers into wolves after they rejected the teachings of Christianity. The disciple of St Columba, St Natalis, is reported to have pronounced a curse on a noble Irish family that meant that every male and female in the family became a wolf for seven years and lived in the woods. Indeed, the 1188 *Topographica Hibernica* written by medieval clergyman and chronicler, Giraldus Cambrensis, tells a story of a priest conversing with a wolf who had suffered such a fate.

St Augustine wrote of werewolves in a very modern manner, almost agreeing with modern psychiatrists when he claimed that, although people may not physically be changed into werewolves, they still believe in their own minds that they are werewolves.

It is very generally believed that by certain witches' spells and the power of the Devil men may be changed into wolves... but they do not lose their human reason and understanding, nor are their minds made the intelligence of a mere beast. Now this must be understood in

St Christopher the Dog-headed Cannibal

Legend has it that around 300 AD, the Romans captured Reprobus, a soldier of the Berber Marmaritae tribe from Cyrene, west of Egypt. The Marmaritae were often described as a dog-headed, cannibalistic tribe. As often happened with captured soldiers, Reprobus was drafted into the Roman army. He also converted to Christianity, adopting the name of Christopher which means 'bearer of Christ'. Sent to Antioch in Syria, he began to convert people to Christianity and was so successful that he was sentenced to death. St Christopher was not a werewolf, however. Nor was he a dog-headed cannibal, except in that the phrase 'dog-headed cannibal' was a Greco-Roman term of abuse reserved for those who lived outside the Roman Empire, especially Africans. There is little doubt that the phrase was associated with his name by scribes writing the early accounts of his life and was taken seriously by later writers as a correct description of how he looked.

this way: namely that the Devil creates no new nature, but that he is able to make something appear to be which in reality is not. For by no spell nor evil power can the mind, nay, not even the body corporeally, be changed into the material limbs and features of any animal... but a man is fantastically and by illusion metamorphosed into an animal, albeit he to himself seems to be a quadruped.

He said this because he wanted to emphasize that only God had the power to create physical beings, whether human or animal. The devil could merely create a perception. Although he is not depicted as a quadruped, the Christian St Christopher, to western Christians the patron saint of travellers, is sometimes depicted in Orthodox religious art with the head of a dog. Was he perhaps a werewolf?

Scene Still from *Silver Bullet*, Daniel Attias, 1985.

WEREWOLF SLAYING

Silver is considered a holy metal that has purifying qualities. Once in contact with a werewolf, it will burn its way into the creature's flesh as well as weaken and confuse it. It is worth noting, however, that the article need not be a silver bullet. Any silver object embedded in the creature's flesh will burn through its hairy layers. There is some debate over whether a silver bullet will finish the werewolf off, but one thing is for sure, silver is the ultimate enemy of the werewolf, so keep some with you at all times.

DEFEATING A WEREWOLF

Quicksilver (a liquid-alloy of mercury and silver) is said to have the power to destroy a werewolf's heart if it is injected into its bloodstream. Religious symbols are famous for warding off any supernatural form of evil such as witches, vampires and of course, werewolves. A silver cross would be particularly potent. If you are really feeling threatened, it would be worth carrying a consecrated host around with you, in the form of a bottle of communion wine or holy water; sprinkle liberally over predator for fatal results. It is also said that a Greek or Turkish Eye charm is anathema to lycanthrops. Werewolves notoriously dislike trees such as mountain ash and rye, therefore mistletoe and wolfsbane can be used to avoid attack. The golden rule of werewolf slaying is, however, that the heart or brain must be destroyed for the animal to die and stay dead. Any other wound will rapidly regenerate over the course of a day, leaving the werewolf free to hunt again.

BERNARD VERLAND

A story from the early 20th century tells of a young man named Bernard Verland who, while walking in the Ardennes Mountains in Belgium, encountered three suspicious looking men whose eyebrows met over the bridge of their noses - a sure sign of werewolves in their human form. Bernard's dog barked and growled at the men and seemed to be frightened of them.

Bernard carried on walking but was conscious that the three men were following close behind. He quickened his pace.

A short while later, he arrived at a dark, secluded spot where the trees grew particularly close to one another. Suddenly, his dog ran off and Bernard followed. As he ran, he could hear the sounds of whining dogs and footsteps running after him. The faster he ran, the closer the footsteps seemed to come. He wondered what he could do to escape and remembered hearing that the mountain ash tree was capable of warding off certain types of evil beings or demons. He looked around, saw one nearby and leapt onto its trunk, climbing up into its lower branches as quickly as he could. He sat there, praying that whatever kind of creatures were pursuing him would react badly to this particular type of tree. As he looked down, the trio of werewolves arrived at the tree, but stopped abruptly at its base. They looked around, snarling angrily but would not approach the tree, let alone try to climb it. They howled with frustration before turning and, to his great relief, running away.

STOPPING AN ATTACK

Werewolves can be released from their spell by being cut on the forehead or struck, in each case three times, by something sharp, ensuring blood is drawn. If you are facing a full frontal attack by a ferocious snarling werewolf it may not be possible, but drawing three drops of blood from the creature with a needle will stop such an attack. Of course, one of the best pieces of advice if you want to remain untouched by werewolfery is to simply avoid dark woods and forests, especially, of course, during a full moon.

THE RISE OF THE WEREWOLF MYTH

The belief in werewolves stems, some say, from the impression made on man in ancient times by the great elemental forces of nature. Everything changed - sun, moon, wind, weather, the seasons and the cycle of life brought the greatest changes of all in birth, adolescence and death. Even gods changed, assuming different shapes as it suited them - Poseidon, Jupiter Ammon, Milosh Kobilitch, Minerva, and countless others.

If all of these changed, then why not man too. Especially, if that change could be used to explain some of the evil that occurs in society, whether it be a serial killer or a serial rapist at whatever period in history. However, some people put forward other causes of the mass werewolf hysteria that gripped Europe for a number of centuries. One theory centres around ergot poisoning. Ergot is a type of fungus that grows on rye grains in certain conditions, most often during wet growing seasons that have followed a very cold winter. It produces alkaloids that can cause the illness known as ergotism in humans and other mammals that eat grain. This illness has been proposed as a believable explanation for possible episodes of werewolfism in Europe in the 18th and 19th centuries.

The symptoms of ergotism are spasms, diarrhea, paresthesias (tingling or numbness of the skin), headaches, nausea and vomiting. However, there can also be hallucinations that are said to be close to those resulting from the ingesting of the psychedelic drug, LSD, which can actually be derived from ergot. Mania and psychosis are often evident. Ergot poisoning has been blamed for individuals believing they were werewolves and also for creating mass hysteria in whole towns causing the inhabitants to believe they have seen a werewolf.

Of course, there are many other reasons for people to have blamed violent, unbelievable events and situations on something supernatural such as werewolves. Serial killing, rape, cannibalism - all of these are difficult to imagine as the work of someone in your own community. What better way to persuade everyone that the evil within a village or town is not human than to find a scapegoat such as a werewolf. It was convenient too to blame strange illnesses that make people behave in an odd, anti-social manner on the easy target of the werewolf, a creature that is being manipulated by unseen outside forces.

MADNESS AND SHAPESHIFTING

The ancients invented the names lycanthropy, kuanthropy or boanthropy to describe a type of madness that made a person believe him or herself to be an animal, each of these reflecting a different shape into which the afflicted person believes he has been turned – a wolf, a dog or a cow, respectively. However, in other parts of the world, local animals were selected as vehicles for shapeshifting. In Europe, the bear was often the preferred shape and in Africa, the hyena or the leopard. The Khands of India spoke of wer-tigers, as did the inhabitants of the tropical forests of Java and Sumatra. In Arawak, wer-jaguars were said to roam the hills.

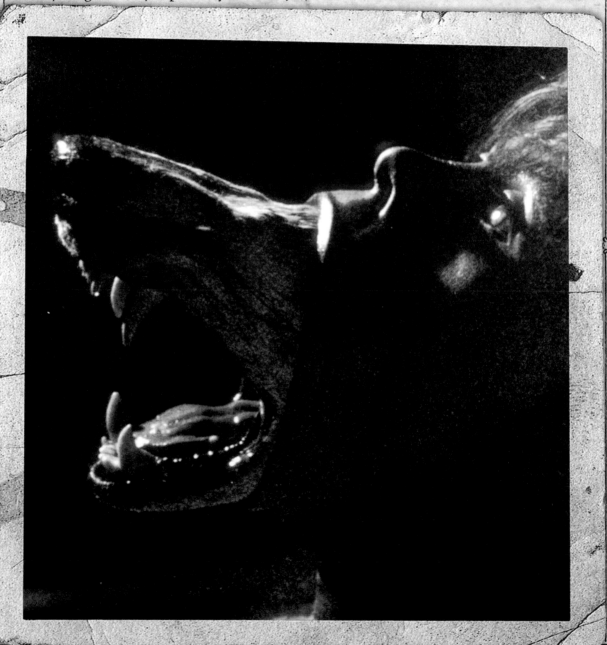

Scene still from *The Company of Wolves*,
Neil Jordan, 1984.

ANCIENT BELIEFS

The legend of the werewolf has its origins in Greek mythology. The very first werewolf is said to have been Lycaon, who lived in Arcadia in the Peloponnese. His story was told in the 2nd century, by Greek traveller and biographer, Pausanias, in the Eighth Book of his *Description of Greece*.

LYCAON AND ZEUS

In ancient times, many worshipped Prometheus, rather than the gods and goddesses of Mount Olympus. Lycaon was overtly antagonistic towards the Olympians who were led by Zeus, cursing them and uttering blasphemies about them. Tiring of Lycaon's attitude, Zeus resolved to teach him a lesson. He travelled to Lycaon's home, to persuade him that he was wrong. Lycaon welcomed him into his house and intimated he was willing to listen. He invited Zeus to dinner so that they could discuss what he needed to do to gain favour with the gods. The arrogant Lycaon had no intention of entering into a proper debate with Zeus, however. Instead, he decided to play a trick on him. He had a dungeon at his house full of people who had wronged him and whom he was powerful and wealthy enough to hold against their will. He selected one of those prisoners and ordered that his throat be cut and his flesh cooked in the stew that was to be eaten that night.

A Gruesome Meal

The meal was put on the table and Lycaon and Zeus sat down to eat. Zeus, however, being an omniscient god, and realizing immediately, therefore, what Lycaon had done, was furious and sent the food flying to the floor. Horrified that his plot had been discovered, Lycaon leapt to his feet and tried to escape. As he ran away, however, he discovered that something odd was happening to him. His fearful cries turned into growls and snarls and he dropped to all fours and began to run. His nose changed into a snout and his ears grew and stretched until they were pointed. His teeth grew like fangs and strangest of all, thick hair began to sprout all over his body.

His Fate is Sealed

It is said that Lycaon actually had the last laugh, because, being a singularly bloodthirsty type anyway, he loved being a werewolf. It allowed him to kill sheep, goats and humans, as he wanted. Eventually, however, the local people tired of his evil

MD·XXIII
AV

The monster Lycaon as described by Pausanias (166 AD) the
werewolf who would sacrifice blood of newborn on altar to revert
to the vulpine states. Engraving by Agostino de Musi, 1523.

deeds and he was exiled to Tatarus. Lycaon's transformation was not for life, however, if he was able to refrain from eating human flesh for nine years. If he succumbed to the desire to eat human flesh, he would remain a wolf forever. Lycaon is said to have lived as a wolf for the remainder of his life.

In Book I of his *Metamorphoses*, the celebrated Roman poet, Ovid, writes of Lycaon:

In vain he attempted to speak; from that very instant

His jaws were bespluttered with foam, and only he thirsted

For blood, as he raged amongst flocks and panted for slaughter.

His vesture was changed into hair, his limbs became crooked;

A wolf, - he retains yet large trace of his ancient expression,

Hoary he is as afore, his countenance rabid,

His eyes glitter savagely still, the picture of fury.

Of course, being a people who lived off the land in rural areas, the Arcadians suffered greatly from attacks by wolves, deliverance from which was secured, they thought, by the sacrifice of a child. This practice was introduced by Lycaon and it is possible that not only the name, lycanthropy, but the entire myth began with him.

ODYSSEY

Homer, in the *Odyssey*, written around the 8th century BC, tells the story of the ten-year journey of the Trojan War hero, Odysseus.

At one point, Odysseus sees smoke rising above the trees of a forest on a small island and he and his men draw lots to see who will go into the forest to investigate. Twenty-three of his men set out and after a while come upon a stone building that is surrounded by mountain wolves and lions. On seeing the men, the animals leap to their feet and run towards them, but they do not attack. They slow down and walk towards them wagging their tails, like domesticated animals. These creatures are actually men who had entered the house of the beautiful goddess Circe who had turned them into werewolves and were-lions. While they have the bodies of animals, they retain the minds of men and are pleased to find some fellow humans.

Neuri Tribe

Ancient Greece also provides us with the story of the Neuri tribe who were said to change into animal form once a year. The Neuri lived in the Bug River basin, west of the Dnieper, in roughly the area of modern day Poland and Belarus. They were known to practice sorcery, although the skeptical Greek historian, Herodotus of Halicarnassus, denied that they possessed shapeshifting powers.

It appears that the Neuri are sorcerers, and such they are held to be by the Scythians and by the Greek settlers in Scythie, who related that once every year each Neurian becomes a wolf for a few days and then again resumes his original form. This, however, they will never persuade me to believe, although they assert it roundly and confirm their statement by a solemn oath.

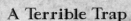 
A Terrible Trap

Of course, the animals are unable to explain all of this to Odysseus's men who are entranced by the beautiful song of the enchantress, Circe. She welcomes them to her house and prepares a meal, but the food contains a drug to make them forget their own homes. She raises her wand - for she is the goddess of magic - and transforms them into swine. In this form, they are pushed outside to join the other animals. One man manages to escape, however, and he runs back to the ship to tell Odysseus what has happened. Odysseus, furious to have apparently lost his men, sets out with a party to free them. En route he is fortunate enough to be intercepted by the god Hermes who provides him with a herb that is an antidote to Circe's drug. Called 'moly', it has a black root and a white flower.

A Clever Trick

The beautiful Circe welcomes the great hero into her home and pours a drink for him in a golden cup. Unknown to him, she puts in the drug that she has already fed to his men. He drinks it and Circe produces her wand, ready to transform him into a pig. She is puzzled, however, when nothing happens. Odysseus has taken the magic herb given to him by Hermes. Odysseus leaps up, his sword at the ready, but at that moment, Circe falls head-over-heels in love with him and invites him to share her bed. Before he does so, however, he insists on her swearing that she will not harm him. Afterwards, Odysseus asks her to free his men from the swine spell she has cast on them and she complies, producing a potion that returns them to human form and brings back their stolen memories. Furthermore, it makes them look younger than before. They sail away, leaving Circe

on her enchanted island with her werewolf and were-lion companions.

PETRONIUS

The first-century Roman author, Petronius wrote the following story in his bawdy work, *The Satyricon*. It is told by a former slave, Niceros, at a dinner party hosted by his friend, Trimalcio:

My master had gone to Capua to sell some old clothes. I took the chance to persuade our guest to keep me company about five miles out of town; for he was a soldier, and as bold as death. We set out about cockcrow, and the moon shone bright as day, when, coming among some monuments my man began to converse with the stars, whilst I jogged along singing and counting them. Presently I looked back after him, and saw him strip and lay his clothes by the side of the road. My heart was in my mouth in an instant, I stood like a corpse; when, in a crack, he was turned into a wolf. Don't think I'm joking: I would not tell you a lie for the finest fortune in the world.

But to continue: after he was turned into a wolf, he began to howl and made straight for the woods. At first I did not know whether I was on my head or my heels; but at last going to take up his clothes, I found them turned into stone. The sweat streamed from me, and I never expected to get over it. Melissa began to wonder why I walked so late. "Had you come a little sooner," she said, "you might at least have lent us a hand; for a wolf broke into the farm and has butchered all our cattle; but though he got off, it was no laughing matter for him, for a servant of ours ran him through with a pike." Hearing this I could not close an eye; but as soon as it was daylight, I ran home like

The Festival of the Wolf

The Lupercalia, the Festival of the Wolf, was held in Rome every year in ancient times between February 13 and 15. It was basically a festival of shepherds, staged in honour of Faunus, the horned god of the forest, plains and fields, who is the Roman equivalent of the Greek god Pan. A statue of Faunus stood in the Lupercal. At this festival, sacrifices were made of a dog and two goats. A feast was held and the goatskins were cut into strips that the Luperci (Brothers of the Wolf) wore around themselves as a belt, after removing their clothing. Holding the hand of another brother, they ran round the old city wall, the naked men being cheered on by the girls and women who lined the route. Each brother wielded a second strip of goatskin that he used to whip the women who competed with each other for the men's attention. It was believed that the goatskin contained the power of the god and that a woman touched by it would easily fall pregnant and be guaranteed the safe and swift delivery of a baby.

The Romans had a word for shapeshifting - *versipellis*, which literally means 'turning the skin', although this can also be used figuratively to mean 'sly' or 'cunning'. From it are derived the English terms 'turncoat' and 'turnskin' for someone who changes sides.

These stories, in particular both versions of the story of Lycaon, have been passed down through the centuries and used and changed by the tellers for their own benefit. They must, consequently be taken with a pinch of salt. However, the fact that the roots of the folkloristic tale of the werewolf reach back into the darkness of ancient history gives comfort to believers and provides non-believers with a fascinating insight into the evolution of a legend.

a pedlar that has been eased of his pack. Coming to the place where the clothes had been turned into stone, I saw nothing but a pool of blood; and when I got home, I found my soldier lying in bed, like an ox in a stall, and a surgeon dressing his neck. I saw at once that he was a fellow who could change his skin and never after could I eat bread with him, no, not if you would have killed me. Those who would have taken a different view of the case are welcome to their opinion; if I tell you a lie, may your guardian spirits confound me!

MARCELLUS SIDETES

The second-century Roman poet Marcellus Sidetes wrote a long medical poem in Greek hexameter verse of which several fragments are extant. One of them, entitled *De Lycanthropia*, claimed that the madness of lycanthropy attacked people generally at the start of a new year. He described how the insanity and the fury would become worse in February and how those afflicted would spend the night in lonely cemeteries, skulking in the dark like ravening dogs and wolves.

Men afflicted with the disease of so-called lycanthropy go out by night in the month of February in imitation of wolves or dogs in all respects, and they tend to hang around tombs till daybreak.

These are the symptoms that will allow you to recognize the sufferers from this disease. They are pallid, their gaze is listless, their eyes are dry and they cannot produce tears. You will observe that their eyes are sunken and their tongue is dry and they are completely unable to put on weight. They feel thirsty, and their shins are covered in lacerations which cannot heal because they are continually falling down and being bitten by dogs. Such are their symptoms.

One must recognize that lycanthropy is a form of melancholia. You will treat it by opening a vein at the time of its manifestation and draining the blood until the time of fainting. Then feed the patient with food conducive to good humours. He is to be given sweet baths. After that, using the whey of the milk, cleanse him over three days with the gourd-medicine of Rufus or Archigenes or Justus. Repeat this a second or third time after intervals.

After the purifications one should use the antidote to viper bites. Take the other measures too prescribed earlier for melancholia. As evening arrives and the disease manifests itself, apply to the head the lotions that usually induce sleep and anoint the nostrils with scents of this sort and opium. Occasionally supply sleep-inducing drinks also.

The great Roman poet, Virgil, wrote:

These herbs of bane to me did Moeris give,
In Pontus culled, where baneful herbs abound.
With these full oft have I seen Moeris change
To a wolf's form, and hide him in the woods,
Oft summon spirits from the tomb's recess,
And to new fields transport the standing corn.

The world of mythology is, of course, replete with characters who changed into beasts of some kind - Jupiter became a bull; Hecuba became a bitch; Actaeon turned into a stag; Ulysses' comrades were changed into swine and the daughters of Proetus ran through the fields believing that they were cows. So convinced were the latter that they were reluctant to let anyone near them in case they put a yoke on them.

PLINY THE ELDER

Pliny the Elder, who lived from around 23 to 79, wrote about werewolves in Book Eight of his wide-ranging work, *Natural History* (*Historia Naturalis*), quoting the Greek author Euanthes as the source for the Arcadian story. He provides a version in which a member of the family of Anthus was chosen by lot every year and taken to a lake where he stripped and hung his clothes on an oak tree. He then swam across the water and on the other side was transformed into a wolf. He spent the next nine years living as a member of a wolf pack. If he succeeded in abstaining from human contact during those nine years, he was able to return to the lake, swim across and then emerge, having regained his human form.

Pliny also mentions an author named Agriopas who told the tale of Demaenetus of Parrhasia who, during the Arcadian sacrifices for the festival of Zeus Lycaeus, ate the entrails of a human child and was turned into a wolf for ten years as punishment. He resumed his human form at the end of those ten years and even competed in the Olympic Games. Pliny, however, was entirely skeptical about the notion of werewolves, putting it alongside a lot of other extravagant tales that had eventually been proven untrue. He did accept, on the other hand, that a lot of people did believe in werewolves and in the ability to experience *versipellis* ('changing the skin').

ROMULUS AND REMUS

One of the most famous of all stories about wolves is that of the feral children, Romulus and Remus, the mythical founders of the city of Rome. According to the version told by the Roman historian Livy (c.59 BC-17 AD), in his book *The History of Rome* (called by him *Ab Urbe Condita*, meaning 'From the City Having Been Founded') Mars, the Roman god of war, forces himself upon the Vestal Virgin, Rhea Silvia, who becomes pregnant by him, even though Vestal Virgins were not supposed to marry or have children. The priestess is imprisoned and gives birth to two sons, named Romulus and Remus, around 771 BC.

The king, Amulius, who has deposed Rhea Silvia's father, is fearful that the two boys will grow up and become rivals for the throne. Amulius orders, therefore, that they be drowned in the nearby River Tiber. At the appointed time, however, the river is in flood and the deepest part cannot be reached (some versions have them being set afloat in a vessel and washed ashore). Instead of being drowned, they are abandoned under a fig tree. The twins' anguished cries are heard by

Romulus and Remus, Charles de La Fosse (1636–1716).

a she-wolf who has come to the riverbank to drink and instead of killing them, she takes pity on them and suckles them on her own milk. She is helped in this by a woodpecker that also brings them food - the woodpecker and the she-wolf, interestingly were both creatures sacred to Mars. Traditionally, she carries the twins in her jaws into a cave on what became known as the 'Lupercal' on the Palatine Hill on which Rome was founded.

The twins are accidentally discovered by Faustulus, a shepherd, who takes them home to his wife, Acca Larentia, and she brings them up as if they are her own. Upon reaching adulthood, the twins kill the usurper, Amulius, and reinstate their grandfather, Numitor, as king of Alba Longa. They subsequently resolve to found their own city and choose as the site the place where the she-wolf had cared for them - the Palatine Hill. As they build the city, the two fall out - some sources say because Remus made fun of the walls that Romulus was building. They fight and Romulus kills his brother. Nevertheless, Romulus continues to build the city, naming it Roma (Rome), after himself.

Statue of the Capitoline Wolf which could date from 5th Century BC. Romulus and Remus, the twins said to be raised by the wolf were added at a later date. Situated at Palazzo dei Conservatori Museum, Rome, Italy.

WOLF ENDS

BRITAIN AND IRELAND

In England, werewolf stories died out as wolves became extinct in the country. King Edgar, who ruled from 959 to 975, is credited with ridding England of wolves. He transformed the annual tribute he was paid by King Idwall of Wales - normally gold and luxuries - into 300 wolf pelts and it is said that within four years there were hardly any wolves left alive, although complete extinction probably did not happen until some time later. In fact, the last wolf in England is reported to have been killed in the 15th century at Wormhill in Derbyshire.

King John the Zombie-Werewolf

One story concerns the unpopular royal personage, King John, known as John 'Lackland' because as his father's youngest son, he did not inherit land out of his family's holdings, and because as king he lost significant amounts of territory to the French. John plundered many churches and monasteries during his reign and at one, the Cistercian Abbey at Swineshead, near Bolton, he gorged himself on peaches that were reputedly poisoned by a monk in revenge for what had been done to the Church. Suffering from dysentery, John was taken to Newark where he died. According to his wishes, he was entombed before the altar of Worcester Cathedral, between the shrines of the two English saints, Oswald and Wulfstan. Shortly after his interment, people were horrified to hear loud shrieks and howls emanating from the tomb. The

Canons of Worcester decided to bring an end to the terrible noise and had the corpse exhumed and re-buried in unconsecrated earth.

To their great disappointment, however, that did not end the matter. Apparently the king was not going to rest in his new grave. There were reports of his hideous, decaying corpse stalking the countryside as a werewolf, terrifying everyone that crossed his path.

The Black Beast of Scotland

The last wolf roaming the hills in Scotland is believed to have been killed in 1743 near Pall-a-chrocain in the Tarnaway Forest in Moray. A 'black beast' had killed a mother and two children, leading the local laird to call in a well-known hunter named Mac-Queen. On the day arranged for the hunt, the laird and his people waited all morning

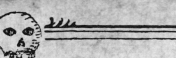
for the famous hunter to put in an appearance. Finally, he appeared, looked around the irritated faces awaiting him and asked them why they were being so impatient. With that, he smiled, opened his bag and removed the bloody head of the wolf that had killed the woman and her children.

The First Werewolf of Merionethshire

The former county of Merionethshire in northwest Wales seems to have been home to at least two werewolves. One story from the early 1930s is told of an Oxford professor and his wife who rented a small cottage in

Last British Wolf, by Harry Johnston, from British Mammals, 1903

the county. While wading in the lake near the cottage, the professor found the skull of what appeared to be a large dog-like creature. He took it home and put it on a shelf in the kitchen.

The next day, the couple were entertaining a guest and the professor and their visitor went out for a walk, leaving the woman alone in the cottage. She already felt uneasy about the skull and her apprehension was increased when she heard a scraping sound at the kitchen door. She thought it might be wise to go into the kitchen and lock the door, but as she did so, she was horrified by the sight of a figure at the window. It had the shape of a man, but its body was hairy and it had the face and angry red eyes of a wolf. Worst of all, it appeared to be trying to get into the cottage. Fortunately, the professor and their guest returned just at that moment and the creature immediately disappeared. When the shaking woman told them what she had seen, they decided to arm themselves, loading a shotgun and fetching some clubs.

Faced with the Beast

A few hours passed before they again heard the sound of scratching at the kitchen window. They leapt to their feet and found themselves staring at a werewolf, its eyes ablaze with bloodlust. However, it turned and fled when it saw them and they set off in pursuit. To their astonishment, it seemed to glide across the ground with superhuman speed that was far too fast for them. It made for the lake and suddenly vanished, not causing a ripple or splash as it entered the water. The next morning, at first light, the professor wisely returned the skull to the exact spot in the lake where he had found it. The werewolf never reappeared.

The Second Werewolf of Merionethshire

Miss St Denis was an artist who was staying on a farm. She was in the habit of setting her easel setting up at the local railway station as the platform there provided the best vantage point for sketching or painting the local countryside. It was a small station with just the one platform and a simple box for a waiting room and booking office. All the station duties were performed by one man and that was all that was required because trains stopped very infrequently.

A Spooky Encounter

One evening, she had been concentrating on her work so much that she neglected to check what the time was. Realizing as she looked at the sky that it was later than usual and that it would soon be getting dark, she hurriedly started to pack her things away. As she did so, however, she was surprised to see a man seated on a truck a few yards from her, staring at her. There was never anyone in the vicinity of the station except on the rare occasion when a train was arriving and, as far as she knew, there was no train due at that time.

An Uneasy Feeling

She suddenly became concerned. The station master's house was about a hundred yards away and beyond that, her lodgings at the farm were the nearest place of safety. Summoning all her courage, she boldly asked the man if he could tell her what time it was, but he remained eerily silent, continuing to stare at her in the gathering gloom. Hurriedly, she finished putting her materials away, gathered her things together, made her way out of the gate and started to walk away from the station, trying to appear as

unconcerned as she could, in the circumstances. A little further on, as she walked she threw a glance over her shoulder. To her horror, she saw that the figure was behind her. She quickened her pace and began to whistle, trying to appear as nonchalant and unconcerned as possible. He continued to follow her. She knew that not far along the road, cliffs would rise on either side, rendering the road almost pitch black and closing her in. Gathering her resolve, she turned round and shouted, 'What do you want? How dare you!' But the words died on her lips because a sudden shaft of fading light splashed across the figure and what she saw filled her with dread.

A Brave Move

The creature had the head of a wolf, covered in shaggy, grey fur. It opened its mouth and displayed long white fangs. It sank down, crouching and ready to pounce. Miss St Denis suddenly remembered that in her pocket was a flashlight that she kept there in case of emergencies. She fumbled in her pocket and found it, bringing it out and switching it on as the creature sprang forward. The light had an immediate effect. The creature shrank back, cowering, putting its paw-like hands over its eyes to block the light. As it did so, it simply, and miraculously, faded away into nothing. Miss St Denis never saw the werewolf again after that night, but made enquiries with the locals soon after. She learned that in one of the quarries close to the place where she had seen the werewolf, some odd bones had been found that were believed to be partly human and partly animal.

IRELAND

Ireland, too, has its werewolf stories, going right back to St Patrick himself. In Ireland, to become a werewolf, a man did not have to be cursed or make a deal with the devil. He could simply be born into a family that had werewolf blood coursing through its veins. It was officially recognized, too. The Late Middle Irish treatise on names, the *Coir Anmann* (Fitness of Names) lists a certain Laignech Faelad who, it says, used to shift into *faelad* (wolf shapes). It adds that he and his children and those that came after him, used to transform themselves into the shapes of wolves and kill the herds. He was given the name Laignech Faelad because, 'he was the first of them to go into wolf-shape.'

The Norse text, the *Konungs Skuggsjá*, written around 1250 for the education of royal princes, speaks of the marvels to be found in Ireland. It talks of a creature that 'was caught in the forest as to which no one could say definitely whether it was a man or some other animal; for no one could get a word from it or be sure that it understood human speech. It had the human shape, however, in every detail, both as to hands and face and feet; but the entire body was covered with hair as the beasts are, and down the back it had a long coarse mane like that of a horse, which fell to both sides and trailed along the ground when the creature stooped in walking.' The last Irish wolf was killed in 1786. He was hunted down near Mount Leinster in County Carlow after savaging a number of sheep. But, although wolves ceased to be a threat to people going about their daily business, werewolf stories still exist from these parts.

The Were Wolves, illustration from
The Book of Werewolves, Sabine Baring-Gould, 1865

FRANCE

France is the spiritual home of the *loup-garou* werewolf and every part of the country seems to have legends of wolf-like creatures terrorizing villages and slaughtering innocent folk.

In the south of France, it was once believed that there were men who transformed themselves into wolves, or *loup-garou*, during the full moon by plunging into a fountain or spring after which they emerged covered in thick fur and walking on all fours. They rampaged across the countryside savaging every living creature they encountered before, at dawn, returning to the spring at which they started out, plunging in again and re-emerging in their human form.

In the Périgord (modern-day Dordogne), the name for a werewolf is *louléerou*. At the full moon, some men, in particular those without a father, make the transformation. Again, immersion in water enables them to make the change. In Normandy, *loup-garou* in their human form, don a skin called the *hère* or *hure* that they have borrowed from the devil. As they roam in their lupine form, they are accompanied by the devil and the only way they can escape this curse is to stab him with a knife three times in the forehead. Some also say that drawing three drops of blood from them with a needle will also release them from being werewolves.

ABBOT GILBERT

In French werewolf lore, not all werewolves are bad. The tale of Abbot Gilbert of the Arc Monastery on the Loire is a fine example of a werewolf going against type.

The abbot had been to a village fair and was riding home to the monastery when he was overcome with drowsiness, helped no doubt by the heat of the summer sun and the fine wine of the village that he had consumed that afternoon. Drifting off to sleep, he slipped from the back of his horse, suffering cuts and bruises, although nothing more serious than that. The scent of his blood, however, was picked up by a herd of wild cats. They fell upon him ferociously and the abbot, being totally unarmed and caught unawares, would have been torn apart by these vicious creatures if it had not been for the intervention of the most unlikely of creatures — a werewolf. The werewolf suddenly appeared from the forest, launched himself at the cats and a battle royal ensued. Gradually, however, he began to gain the upper hand, although he was bitten and badly cut, he succeeded in sending the hissing and spitting cats packing.

Apprehensive Abbot

The werewolf decided to accompany the abbot back to the safety of the monastery. The abbot was reluctant to be seen in the company of such a creature, even though he had saved his life, and protested that he did not have to, but the werewolf insisted. At the monastery, although at first afraid, the monks, on hearing how the creature had saved their abbot's life, tended to his wounds and befriended him.

The next morning, when they awoke, the monks and the abbot were astonished to find that the werewolf had returned to his human form and even more astonished to learn that he was, in fact, a Church dignitary of some standing. He delivered a lecture to the abbot for allowing himself to behave in the unseemly manner of the previous day, ordering him to undergo penance that was so bad that the abbot eventually resigned from his position.

ROLAND BERTIN

André Bonivon was the captain of a schooner called the *Bonaventure* that was attacking Huguenot (French Protestant) settlements along the Gulf of Lions in southern France during the reign of Louis XIV. On one raid, Bonivon sailed up the Rhone estuary further than he had intended and ran ashore. A storm suddenly got up and in the general panic that ensued, Bonivon found himself in the water, trapped in a treacherous whirlpool. Just when he thought his end was near, he felt someone grab him, divest him of his heavy coat that was pulling him under and drag him onto dry land. Relieved to be alive, he stuck out his hand to his rescuer but was horrified to have it taken by a large hairy paw-like hand.

He immediately believed he had been rescued by the devil and threw himself to his knees pleading for God's forgiveness. His rescuer silently pulled him to his feet and led him inland to a house on the outskirts of a small town. He signalled for him to enter but Bonivon was immediately struck by a sickly stench. Reluctantly, he was led to a room and when his rescuer appeared carrying a lantern, Bonivon saw his face for the first time and realized that he was in the company of a werewolf. Terrified, he tried to escape, but stumbled and fell, only to be helped to his feet once more by the creature which led him to a table laid out with food.

A Grisly Discovery

After he had eaten, the werewolf left him, locking the door behind him and Bonivon explored his prison. He tried the window but was unable to shift the sturdy iron bars that guarded it. Then, to his horror, he discovered the mutilated body of a woman lying on the floor, concealed by a curtain. Was that the fate, he wondered with a chill, that awaited him?

He was, of course, unable to sleep and sat dreading the return of his captor. Shortly after dawn, footsteps approached and the door swung open. Bonivon anxiously awaited his fate, but instead of a werewolf, there facing him was the figure of a man. Not only that, he was dressed as a Huguenot minister.

A Witch's Spell

Bonivon laughed uncontrollably in relief and when he had stopped the minister began to talk. He told him that he was in the house of Roland Bertin and the dead woman in the corner was his wife. Bonivon's crew had viciously murdered her during one of their raids the previous day, he continued, and he had been taken prisoner to be tortured and drowned at sea. Bonivon began to recognize the man as a prisoner on his ship. Bertin explained that he had been transformed into a werewolf by a witch in the village. As soon as darkness had fallen the previous day, he had metamorphosed and had leapt ashore with everyone else when the ship had run aground. However, he had seen Bonivon in trouble and had turned back to save him instead of trying to escape.

He had no idea why he had done it, why he had saved the man who had been responsible for his wife's death and for pillaging his home and town. He explained that he did it probably because he loved all living things. He told the captain, 'Murderer, I have spared you. Now you spare others.' The captain could not fail to be moved and from that time on he was a changed man. He never harmed another Huguenot.

HENRI SANGFEU

In a village not far from Blois, an innkeeper had a very pretty daughter, Beatrice. She was admired by many young men, but two were particularly tenacious, handsome Herbert Poyer, and Henri Sangfeu who was a nice but plain-looking boy. To Henri's intense disappointment, but no one's surprise, Beatrice chose to marry Herbert.

Cruel Taunts

Henri was very upset, but his anguish was made worse by a poem that caricatured him and made fun of his looks. The poem spread around the village and he was humiliated. Even Beatrice laughed at him and he began to hate her as passionately as he had once loved her. He grew angry and thought long and hard about how he could make the villagers, and even his dear Beatrice, pay.

Out for Revenge

He had heard about a witch who lived in the forest, known as Mère Maxim, who had been accused of starting several epidemics in the village, of causing accidents and more than one death. It was dangerous to venture anywhere near her hut in the forest, but Henri wanted revenge so badly that he discounted all the tales he had been told and, making sure the sun was shining brightly, made his way into the forest to find her.

Finding the Witch

To his surprise, however, Mère Maxim was no old hag. In fact, she was an attractive woman with dark hair, rosy cheeks and gleaming white teeth. He was less taken with her eyes, which occasionally seemed to have a glint of something unpleasant in them, and she had long curved nails. Before long, he was seated beside her in her hut kissing her at her invitation. She told him that he was indeed far from handsome, but he was fat and she liked fat boys.

A Cunning Plan

She made sure that no one knew he was there and advised him to treat Beatrice with civility and friendliness. She then gave him a couple of items that he should give Beatrice as a wedding present - a beautiful belt that was made from the skin of a wild animal and a box of pink and white sugar plums. She ordered him to present them to Beatrice on the night before the wedding and as soon as he had done so to come and see her. He left her after another kiss, his heart pounding, longing for it to be the wedding eve so that he could come back and see her once again. Back in the village the taunts about his ugliness continued, but they meant nothing to him any more. He was in love.

On the night before the wedding, he did as he had been instructed. He handed Beatrice her presents and then hurried off into the forest for another assignation with Mère Maxim. It was night time, however, and the forest seemed a very different place. He was frightened and even thought he was being watched by a strange figure in the trees as he made his way along the path. He saw a face amongst the branches, a face that he could not tell if it was human or animal, or perhaps something else. Mère Maxim was waiting for him, more beautiful to his eyes than ever. He lay in her arms in her hut and she kissed him and stroked his cheeks and arms, commenting on how deliciously fat they were. She then fetched a length of rope and began to bind his hands and feet. Meanwhile, drowsy with love, he let her.

The Witch's True Identity

At each knot she tied, she laughed and finally she bound him to the seat. He could not break free. She then sat beside him and undid the clothes around his chest and throat. She told him, 'By this time, your pretty Beatrice will have worn the belt and eaten the sweets. She is now a werewolf!' She went on to explain to him how the cursed girl would creep out of her house every night at midnight and hunt for a weak old woman, or a baby, 'always someone fat, tender and juicy, like you!' With that, she bent low over him, bared her teeth and sank her long, sharp nails deep into his ample flesh. A log on the fire spat and a sudden flame cast a light across the room onto her face.

With increasing horror, Henri realized that he was not looking at the face of a human being. But, by then, it was too late.

JEAN GRENIER

The name Garnier or Grenier is often associated with werewolves. Jean Grenier was tried for being a werewolf in the Landes area near Bordeaux in 1603. Just 14 years of age, Grenier was a shepherd but when the time came for him to effect a transformation into a werewolf, he would take himself off to a remote location. He would return, bent on murder and mayhem, hunting women and children.

A little girl named Marguerite Poirier tended sheep with Grenier but she often came home and told her parents that he had terrified her with the stories he told. He had, he told her, sold his soul to the devil in order to acquire the power of becoming a wolf. He roamed the countryside in search of victims and, although he had mostly killed dogs, he also claimed to have killed a couple of little girls. In one case, he had eaten as much of her as he could and the remainder he had tossed to a wolf. In the second instance, he had drunk her blood and had eaten everything apart from her arms and shoulders.

Disappearance of Girls

Then, one day, when she was on her own watching the sheep, Marguerite was attacked by a wolf. She had used her shepherd's crook to fight him off and had fled. The wolf, she said, was a little shorter and fatter than normal, had red hair, a stumpy tail and a head that seemed smaller than that of a normal wolf. The villagers were deeply concerned, especially as several young girls had

mysteriously disappeared recently. Parents began to keep their children indoors and the authorities in Bordeaux were informed. Jean Grenier was brought before a court of investigation.

Monsieur de la Forest

He told how he had been born the son of a poor labourer and had, since leaving home, been doing odd jobs for several people, although he had been dismissed from employment several times for neglecting his duties. He then went on to claim that, at the age of 10 or 11, his neighbour, Monsieur Duthillaire, had introduced him to a mysterious man in the depths of a forest. This man, 'Monsieur de la Forest' had marked him with a fingernail and had given him some lotion and a wolfskin. He claimed that from that time onward, after he had smeared his body with the lotion and donned the wolfskin, he had been able to roam the countryside whenever he wanted in the guise of a wolf. He admitted that his intention had been to kill and devour Marguerite Poirier, that only her courage in fighting him off with her staff had stopped him.

A List of Crimes

He further admitted to taking a baby from a house in a village and eating as much as he could before throwing the remainder to a wolf. He had also killed and eaten a little girl in a black dress as she tended to a flock of sheep in his home parish of St Antoine de Pizon. In the same parish, six weeks previously, he had killed another child. He claimed that he hunted children on the orders of 'Monsieur de la Forest' whom he called his master or the Lord of the Forest. He accused his father of having also taken part in his nightly excursions and

attributed his father and mother's separation to the fact that she had once witnessed her husband vomit the paws of a dog and some fingers of a child. His father was later exonerated, however.

Werewolf in the Court

When the facts he had given regarding his attacks on the little girls were investigated, the places, dates and times were found to be correct, as were the types of wounds he inflicted on his victims. A man who had interrupted him while he was attacking a little boy, was found and he corroborated what Grenier had told the court about the incident. In summing up the case, the president of the court announced that he was paying no heed to the stories of supernatural occurrences, transformations and devilish involvement. Instead, he emphasized the age and lack of intelligence of the boy as well as his lack of education and the neglect he had suffered at the hands of his parents. He denied the existence of lycanthropy, astutely pointing out that, as it was something that occurred only in the mind, it could not, therefore, be punished by a court of law. Jean Grenier was sentenced to life imprisonment in a monastery in Bordeaux where he is reported to have run about on all fours like a wolf and eaten raw meat. He died aged 20.

Interestingly, the attitude of the courts to lycanthropy seemed to be changing around this time. As was demonstrated by the president of the court in the Grenier trial, it was beginning to be looked upon as a malady of the mind, rather than a crime that could be punished in a court of law.

GILLES GARNIER

Born in Lyons, Gilles Garnier became known as the Hermit of Dôle, the town near which he lived. Garnier, who was executed for his crimes on 18 January 1573, confessed after his capture to having made a pact with the devil one night while roaming in the forest where he lived. He was given the power to transform himself into a wolf with the help of a lotion with which he was supplied. He thought it would help him hunt for game to feed himself and his family. Unfortunately, the game he began to hunt was often not animal.

His First Murder

Just after the Feast of St Michael, Garnier was in the form of a wolf and prowling around a vineyard when a girl walked in. He seized and killed the 10-year-old, dragging her into the cover of nearby woods, ripping her clothing from her body and devouring her flesh, taking what he did not eat home for his wife and children. On another occasion, he had to abandon an attempt to abduct another little girl when he was interrupted by a group of people. A week later, he killed a little boy, ate the flesh off his thighs and stomach and ripped off a leg to take home.

Garnier was eventually caught when he attacked a child without assuming his lupine form. He was seen and recognized by some people working in the vicinity. He and his wife were arrested and charged with murder. Garnier's defence was that he was a victim of a force greater than himself and the court concurred that he had indeed been the victim of supernatural forces, but they concluded that this fact did not lessen the severity of his crimes. They found him guilty and decided to make an example of him. People had to learn what would happen to them if they tampered with the forces of evil or made so-called pacts with the devil. They sentenced him to be purged by fire and he suffered the horrific fate of being burned alive at the stake.

DEMON TAILOR

Just over 20 years after the execution of Gilles Garnier, there was another notorious werewolf case in France, in Châlons, near Paris. In December 1598, the 'Werewolf of Châlons' - also known as the 'Demon Tailor' - was arraigned on murder charges that were so horrific that all the documents relating to the case were destroyed after the trial.

A Barbaric Tailor

The man, whose name has not been passed down through the centuries, was a tailor in Paris who would often lure children into his shop. There he would assault them sexually and torture them before cutting their throats. He would then cut them up, cook the pieces and eat them. Sometimes, when he was unable to locate victims in that way, he was reported to stalk the woods in wolf form, hunting for children. It is thought that he killed more than 20 children using these methods.

When rumours about him reached the ears of officials, his premises were raided and in the basement were found barrels filled with bleached bones and other human remains.

The tailor was convicted and sentenced to burn at the stake, and as they set light to the logs on which he stood, he still displayed no remorse. In fact, he is reported to have cursed and blasphemed until the flames were licking around his body. The large crowd divined from his reaction that he had indeed made a pact with the devil.

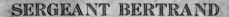

SERGEANT BERTRAND

The case of Sergeant Bertrand was the last authenticated case of its kind. It was 1847 and for a number of months, Parisian cemeteries had been regularly violated. Suspicion had fallen on cemetery owners, local police officers, and even the relatives of the dead.

The famous cemetery of Père Lachaise was the first to be attacked. People claim to have seen a creature that they described as partly human and partly animal moving amongst the gravestones. They tried to get close to it, but it always vanished. Dogs, meanwhile, became terrified when in the creature's vicinity. In the mornings they would find graves dug up, coffin lids ripped off and the cadavers showing signs of having been bitten and eaten. Doctors who examined them reckoned that the bodies had been eaten with human teeth.

It spread. The body of a recently buried little girl was found half-eaten. The guard on the cemetery was doubled, but it happened again a number of times, despite the high walls and iron gates.

One part of the wall showed signs of having recently been climbed and so a trap was set at that point, with a wire connected to some explosives. At midnight, a loud bang was heard and as guards converged on the scene, they saw the figure of a man disappearing over the top of the wall. Blood was found soaked on torn pieces of military uniform near the scene of the explosion. They now knew that their quarry was a soldier.

A Soldier's Confession

The next day, it was reported that a sergeant of the 74th Regiment had been taken to hospital the previous night, badly wounded. When investigated, the sergeant, whose name was Bertrand, confessed to being the person they were looking for. He told them that he had been driven against his will by an unknown force to carry out the attacks on the cemeteries. In one night, he admitted, he had exhumed and bitten fifteen bodies. He described himself at those times as like a wild animal, tearing up the earth with his bare hands and ripping off the coffin lids. He added that, following the attacks, he felt inordinately tired and would fall into a deep sleep, sometimes even before he made it home. During those sleeps, he said he felt a peculiar transformation taking place in his body.

Questioned further, he told investigators that he preferred the company of animals to other children when he was young, and that he used to frequent remote places - moors, woods and deserts - in order to commune with animals. He described how after one such excursion he first experienced the feel-

The Gandillon Family

In 1598, a family named Gandillon were tried. Pernette Gandillon, believing herself to be a werewolf, attacked two children, one of whom survived and identified her as the attacker. She was attacked by an angry mob and torn to pieces. They then accused Pierre, her brother, of being a witch and a shapeshifter. He and his son - probably under torture - confessed to being in possession of an ointment that helped them to effect the transformation into wolves. Scars were found on their bodies that were presumed to have been received when they were in wolf form and had engaged in fights with dogs.

As often seems to have been the case, it is reported that once they were imprisoned, Pierre and his son began to walk around on all fours, like wolves, and could often be heard howling.

ing of changing while asleep. The following morning, he sneaked into a cemetery and watched some gravediggers tending to a grave. When it started to rain, the gravediggers had gone off to take shelter and he felt an overwhelming desire to open the coffin and take a bite at the body inside. He was interrupted on that occasion, but since that time had been unable to resist the temptation that came upon him after sunset. Doctors declared Bertrand to be sane, but believed that he had been overcome by a mania of some kind. He was sentenced to one year in prison and after he was released, was never heard of again.

THE BEAST OF GÉVAUDAN

Gévaudan is a mountainous district in Lozere in southern France where wolves have always been fairly common. Indeed, the incidents that launched one of the most famous of all cases of werewolf hysteria began with a wolf attack.

In June 1764, a woman was tending her cattle near a village named Langogne when she was attacked by a large ferocious wolf. Her cattle, panicked by the creature, stampeded and the wolf was forced to run off before finishing his work. The following month, on 3 July, a 14-year-old girl was killed and partially eaten close to the village of Habats and on 8 August, another girl was found dead. The partially-eaten bodies of two boys were found at the start of September.

The Creature's Modus Operandi

It appeared that the creature that had killed them had used the same method each time. It had made a frontal attack and when they were on the ground, had bitten them savagely in the face and neck, decapitating them. It continued. On 6 September, a woman was found dead and by the end of October, five more children were discovered dead and brutally torn to pieces.

The people of Gévaudan were understandably terrified. The belief grew that they were being stalked by a *loup-garou*, a werewolf. A brief interlude in the killings suggested that the creature may have been mating, but on 25 November, an old woman was found dead, her face ripped open. A number of other attacks followed and at the end of the month two children were killed in Auvergne. The authorities responded by sending a dragoon of guards from Clermond-Ferrand with orders to hunt the beast down. Although they succeeded in killing 74 wolves in the local forests, it became apparent that their prey was not amongst them when a young boy was killed on Christmas Eve, followed by a shepherd two days later. Two more bodies, both little girls, were discovered, partially eaten, like all the rest, before the end of December.

The Spree Continues

Prayers were said by the local bishop as another three bodies turned up at the beginning of the new year and on 12 January the wolf attacked seven children at the village of Villaret. The bigger children succeeded, however, in chasing it away. But by the middle of the month, it had claimed several more victims. Three men, who were attacked on 18 January, were able to provide a description of the creature. They described it as huge, but extremely agile. It could rear up on its hind legs, somewhat like a bear, but at other times, it attacked from an all-fours position. Some began to question whether

Illustration of a werewolf hunt, France, 19th Century

it was a wolf or something more sinister and supernatural. By the end of January it had mutilated another three people.

Hunting the Beast

The men of the area started a search of the forest in which the wolf was believed to roam. Some 20,000 men hunted down every wolf they could find and many were killed, but the killer was not amongst them because on 1 February, a young man was attacked near Marvejols, although he was lucky; his life was saved by his dog. A girl of 14 was decapitated on 9 February. The French king, Louis XV, became extremely concerned about the mayhem in the south and put a price on the creature's head. He sent a famous hunter named Donneval to Gévaudan to finally rid the area of the fiend, which, if anything, seemed to be increasing the frequency of its attacks. It was now being described as being as tall as a calf, extraordinarily long for a wolf and of a reddish colour with a brown streak running down its back. It also had a huge tail. This was no ordinary wolf.

Attacks continued through the first five months of 1765, with around a dozen people being killed and eaten while the hunter Donneval scoured the area with a pack of hounds. He took care of another 19 wolves, but as the beast's strikes continued, it was evident that it was still roaming the hills. On 21 September, a huge wolf was shot and wounded by another hunter that the king had dispatched to the region. It fell, but staggered to its feet and tried to escape. Another bullet struck it, however, and it ran for a short distance before finally collapsing.

A Giant Werewolf

When they approached it, they discovered it was massive. Several of the people who had survived its attacks identified it as the beast and, as everyone breathed a huge sigh of relief, it seemed that, at last, after more than a year of terror, the nightmare was finally over. Sadly, it was not. On 10 December a youth was injured in an attack and by the end of the month the killing had resumed as before, two small girls being found dead and savaged.

It continued until June 1767, three years after it had begun, when 300 hunters gathered in the forest of La Ténazeire and were posted amongst the trees. One of them, a man of 60, named Jean Chastel, was waiting intently when a huge beast broke from cover. Without hesitation, Chastel took aim and fired, killing the beast with his second silver bullet. When they examined the carcass, it looked like the creature they were hunting, and its identity was confirmed when its stomach was opened and found to contain the shoulder bone of a girl who had been attacked just 24 hours previously.

The attacks ceased and Gévaudan was at last able to return to normal. The death toll had reached 113 and 49 people had been injured. The creature's body started to rapidly putrefy and it was disposed of, one story saying it was buried somewhere in the forest while another said it was burned.

In the Middle Ages, large bands of beggars and brigands took full advantage of the werewolf hysteria by roaming remote areas of Europe clad in wolfskins and howling as if they were a pack of wolves out hunting. They were called 'werewolves' and perhaps that was a lexicographical throwback to the old Norwegian word *vargulf* that means literally, 'rogue wolf'.

THE TALE OF BISCLAVRET

Bisclavret is one of twelve tales written by Marie de France in the 12th century. The story has been passed down for generations, and it is unknown whether it is a true account or a work of fiction.

Bisclavret is a baron in the Brittany region of France and every week he disappears for three days and no one - not even his wife - knows where he goes. Eventually, his curious wife pleads with him to tell her what happens during those three days and he explains that he is, in fact, a werewolf. He describes how he takes off his clothes and transforms but explains how in order to be able to return to his human form, he requires his clothing. He hides it very carefully, therefore, in a hollow rock, where his clothes will not be discovered.

Bisclavret is unaware that his wife is having an affair with a knight. She summons her lover, tells him about her husband's curse and sends him out to find the hollow rock and steal her husband's clothes while he is roaming the countryside in his lupine form. Bisclavret returns to the hollow rock as usual but finds his clothes gone. Unable to resume his human shape, he cannot return home. In time, claiming her husband to be dead, Bisclavret's wife marries the knight and moves into his castle.

A year later, the king, who is visiting the area, is out hunting when his dogs encounter and corner a strange wolf-like creature. It is, of course, Bisclavret who, when he sees the king, runs to him and pleads for mercy, lavishing kisses on the monarch's leg and foot as he sits astride his horse. The king is taken aback and wondering what nature of creature this is, orders that the dogs be restrained. He and his party are astonished by the wolf's apparent gentleness and nobility.

He decides to take Bisclavret back to his palace and allow him to live there.

A Revenge Attack

Some time later, the knight who had married Bisclavret's wife pays a visit to the royal court. When he has an audience with the king, however, the wolf Bisclavret, who is present, attacks him. It seems so uncharacteristic of the normally placid creature that everyone at court immediately believes that the knight must have wronged him in the past. Curious, the king decides to visit the part of Brittany where the knight now lives and when Bisclavret's wife appears at the gates of her castle to welcome the royal party, Bisclavret also attacks her, savaging her and biting off her nose.

Torture and Interrogation

When the king enquires into the castle's recent history, someone tells him about the disappearance of the baron, Bisclavret. Becoming suspicious, the king orders that Bisclavret's wife be tortured. Before long, she confesses everything and informs the king where her husband's clothing can be found. When the clothing is put before the wolf, however, he ignores it. Someone suggests that he should be given privacy to change and he is allowed to use a bed camber to don the clothing and effect his transformation back to human form.

All ends happily with Bisclavret being restored to his former possessions and his wife and her knight being exiled. It is said that many of the exiled wife's female children were afterwards born without noses.

GUILLAUME DE PALERME

The romance poem, *Guillaume de Palerme*, composed around 1200, recounts the story of Alfonso, heir to the Spanish throne. Alfonso is turned into a werewolf by his stepmother, Braunde, using a magic potion. Although a werewolf, however, Alfonso retains his human mind. He snatches a baby from Palermo in Sicily and swims with the boy to mainland Italy. What Alfonso does not know, however, is that the child is Guillaume, son of the king.

The Boy is Stolen

Nonetheless, the wolf brings the boy up, caring for him, but one day when he is out foraging for food for the boy, a cowherd happens upon the boy and steals him. Alfonso learns where Guillaume is and is happy that he seems to have been found by a caring, human parent. He decides to leave him there as he considers the boy to be better off. Then one day, while out hunting, the Emperor of Rome becomes separated from the rest of the royal party and gets lost. He meets Guillaume who is out in the forest and is very impressed by him, so impressed, in fact, that he lifts him up onto his horse and takes him back to his palace. Guillaume is appointed pageboy to the emperor's daughter, Melior.

Reunited

As time passes, Guillaume and Melior fall in love but as she is destined to marry a Greek prince, they flee into the woods, clad in bearskins to disguise themselves. They wander for a while but gradually begin to starve. Fortunately, however, they meet Alfonso the werewolf who goes out to hunt for food and, having robbed some travellers he had encountered, returns with food and wine. He feeds them and then helps them to make their way to Sicily.

By this time, Guillaume's father is dead and the Spanish king is threatening to conquer the country. Guillaume leads the Sicilian army against him, on his shield the heraldic device of a werewolf, 'hideous and huge, with all his correct and most suitable colour, so to be obvious in the field; other (coat of) arms, in all my life, I'll never have.' Guillaume triumphs over the Spanish army and wins back his kingdom. Alfonso becomes disenchanted by Braunde and returns to his human form.

Engraving showing a werewolf devouring a young woman, circa 1901.

GERMANY

France has certainly had a lot of werewolves, but Germany has probably had more, to such an extent that preachers delivered sermons about them. One extraordinary sermon, given in 1508, demonstrates how seriously the Church took the werewolf threat.

What shall we say about were-wolves? For there are were-wolves which run about the villages devouring men and children. As men say about them, they run about full gallop, injuring men, and are called ber-wölff, or wer-wölff. Do you ask me if I know aught about them?

I answer, Yes. They are apparently wolves which catch men and children, and that happens on seven accounts:

1. Esuriem   Hunger.
2. Rabiem   Savageness.
3. Senectutem Old age.
4. Experientiam Experience.
5. Insaniem   Madness.
6. Diabolum   The Devil.
7. Deum   God.

The first happens through hunger; when the wolves find nothing to eat in the woods, they must come to people and eat men when hunger drives them to it. You see well, when it is very cold, that the stags come in search of food up to the villages, and the birds actually into the dining-room in search of victuals.

Under the second head, wolves eat children through their innate savageness, because they are savage...Their savageness arises first from their condition. Wolves which live in cold places are smaller on that account, and more savage than other wolves. Secondly, their savageness depends on the season; they are more savage about Candlemas than at any other time of the year, and men must be more on their guard against them then than at other times. It is a proverb, "He who seeks a wolf at Candlemas, a peasant on Shrove Tuesday, and a parson in Lent, is a man of pluck." . . . Thirdly, their savageness depends on their having young. When the wolves have young, they are more savage than when they have not...

Under the third head, the wolves do injury on account of their age. When a wolf is old, it is weak and feeble in its legs, so it can't ran fast enough to catch stags, and therefore it rends a man, whom it can catch easier than a wild animal. It also tears children and men easier than wild animals, because of its teeth, for its teeth break off when it is very old...

Under the fourth head, the injury the were-wolves do arises from experience. It is said that human flesh is far sweeter than other flesh; so when a wolf has once tasted human flesh, he desires to taste it again. So he acts like old topers, who, when they know the best wine, will not be put off with inferior quality.

Under the fifth head, the injury arises from ignorance. A dog when it is mad is also inconsiderate, and it bites any man; it does not recognize its own lord: and what is a wolf but a wild dog which is mad and inconsiderate, so that it regards no man.

Under the sixth head, the injury comes of the Devil, who transforms himself, and takes on him the form of a wolf. So writes Vincentius in his *Speculum Historiale*. And he has taken it from Valerius Maximus in the Punic war. When the Romans fought against the men of Africa, when the captain lay asleep, there came a wolf and drew his sword, and carried it off. That was the Devil in a wolf's form. The like writes William of Paris, that a wolf will kill and devour children, and do the greatest mischief. There was a man who had the phantasy that he himself was a wolf. And afterwards he was found lying in the wood, and he was dead out of sheer hunger.

Under the seventh head, the injury comes of God's ordinance. For God will sometimes punish certain lands and villages with wolves. So we read of Elisha, that when Elisha wanted to go up a mountain out of Jericho, some naughty boys made a mock of him and said, 'O bald head, step up! O glossy pate, step up!' What happened? He cursed them. Then came two bears out of the desert and tore about forty-two of the children. That was God's ordinance. The like we read of a prophet who would set at naught the commands he had received of God, for he was persuaded to eat bread at the house of another. As he went home he rode upon his ass. Then came a lion which slew him and left the ass alone. That was God's ordinance. Therefore must man turn to God when He brings wild beasts to do him a mischief: which same brutes may He not bring now or evermore. Amen.

As a result of this fascination with lycanthropy, Germany has had its share of werewolf stories, but probably none is better known than that of Peter Stubbe who was executed at Bedburg on 31 March 1590. Copies of a pamphlet that can be found in Lambeth Library and the British Museum show the extent to which his heinous crimes were publicized at the time. It starts:

A true Discourse
Declaring the damnable life
and death of one Stubbe Peeter,
a most Wicked Sorcerer, who in the
likeness of a Woolfe, committed many
murders, continuing this Divelish practice
25 Years, killing and devouring Men,
Women, and Children

The pamphlet details his crimes as they were presented at his trial, but of course, may be taken with a pinch of salt, given that the information was in all likelihood gained through torture.

PETER STUBBE

Peter Stubbe (sometimes Peter Stumpp) was born in the village of Epprath, near the town of Bedburg in Germany's Cologne region. His murderous reign on the area lasted 25 years, killing 18 people and mutilating countless others during that time.

It is said that at a very early age he had already made a pact with the devil that guaranteed him anything he wanted. All he wanted, it seems, was to acquire the power to change into a wolf's form and kill women and children. To effect this, the devil provided him with a wolf-hair girdle or belt. As soon as Stubbe fastened the belt around his waist, he was transformed into a

Illustration showing Peter Stubbe, 'The Werewolf
of Bedburg' being executed at Bedburg, near Köln,
Germany, 1589.

huge and ferocious wolf with blazing eyes and powerful jaws filled with strong, sharp fangs. Removing the belt instantly turned him back into human form.

The Terror Begins

Over a period of 25 years, a series of unexplained murders took place in Bedburg. Bodies would turn up savagely mutilated. Often, it would emerge later, they were people with whom Peter Stubbe had argued, although he was not averse to ripping out the throat of a young girl when the urge came over him.

Over the course of a few years, he murdered 13 children and also killed two pregnant women, savagely ripping their unborn babies from their wombs. Evidence was found that he tore the hearts of his victims from their bodies shortly after death and devoured them. Even his own family was not safe. One day when he was working with his son in the fields, he donned his wolf-hair girdle and killed the boy. He split open his skull, scooped out the still warm brains and ate them. He forced himself on his daughter and incestuously fathered a child by her.

He was finally caught in 1589 after attacking a group of children playing in a field in which there was a large herd of cows. Stubbe had attacked, having singled out one little girl, but she was wearing a thick collar and it prevented him from sinking his teeth into her neck. As they struggled, the other children screamed and shouted so loudly that the cows panicked and stampeded, frightening the werewolf off. The villagers, hearing the commotion, poured from their houses and immediately formed a search party. Using mastiff hounds, they quickly tracked him down and surrounded him. Trapped, Stubbe, still in his lupine form, disappeared from sight into some bushes where he tore off his wolf-hair girdle. Suddenly the trackers saw Peter Stubbe emerge from the wolf's hiding place, strolling along as if nothing untoward had occurred.

The Beast is Captured

They were not fooled, however, and seized him. He was dragged to the magistrates at Bedburg where he confessed under torture to having made his pact with the devil that permitted him to adopt 'the likeness of a greedy, devouring wolf, strong and mighty, with eyes great and large, which in the night sparkled like fire, a mouth great and wide, with most sharp and cruel teeth, a huge body, and mighty paws'.

Found Guilty

He was found guilty of cannibalism and incest and even of having had intercourse with a succubus (a female demon) sent to him by the devil. He was sentenced to death and endured one of the most brutal executions imaginable. He was tortured on the rack and then on a wheel, with heated pincers being used to strip off his flesh in ten different places on his body. His limbs were then broken with blows by wooden mallets to prevent him returning from the grave. He was then decapitated and his body was burned on a pyre, his wife and daughter, also arrested as alleged member of his pack, looking on before they too were burned. Stubbe's head was put on display to deter others. The villagers searched long and hard for the wolf-hair girdle that they believed he must have thrown away just before he was captured, but it was nowhere to be found. They said the devil must have reclaimed his property.

COUNT VON BREBER

The Police Chief of the town of Magdeburg, Count von Breber, was travelling in the Harz Mountains with his young wife, Hilda. They were making for the village of Grautz where they planned to spend the night when a strange thing happened.

The road led them over a small stream, but when they came to it, their dogs seemed to be extremely reluctant to cross it, cowering and whimpering when they approached it. Having carried them across, they finally arrived at Grautz where the Count told the innkeeper of the dogs' strange behaviour, describing the spot on the road. The innkeeper was visibly shaken, explaining that this spot, guarded by two giant poplars, was known as Wolf Hollow. He told the Count that it was believed locally that drinking the waters of the stream at that point did odd things to people. Being a practical man, the Count was sceptical. After all, his wife had scooped up only a handful of the water and drunk it. If she heard this nonsense, he realized, she would be very distressed. He made the innkeeper swear to say nothing about this to her.

Frightening Nightmares

Not long after, when Count von Breber and his wife returned to their estate near Magdeburg, Hilda began to have strange, frightening nightmares. The bad dreams began to haunt her but she did not tell her husband. Gradually, she began to go off her food and her health began to suffer. Worried about her, and wanting to allow her to sleep peacefully, the Count moved into the bedroom next door.

Missing Children

As Police Chief, however, he had plenty of other things to worry him. Children, mostly from poor families, had recently been disappearing in the town. When the children of important people also began to disappear, he had to do something. He ordered his men out to search every street in Magdeburg for the missing children. One night, when he was sitting at home, pondering the problem, an irate woman came to his door. Her child had vanished and she was certain that it had not been a human who had taken the child, but a monster of some kind. The Count sent her packing but she had set him thinking and he decided to follow her.

Half-woman, half-wolf

Out in the street, the Count saw the woman and in front of her another dark figure that seemed to be that of a woman, carrying a sack. Martha shouted suddenly that this was the creature that had abducted her child. The woman ran off with Martha following and von Breber in hot pursuit. They ran on to some waste ground that the Count did not recognize and ahead of them was a building into which the first woman ran with Martha close behind her. Von Breber stumbled and fell and as he started to painfully get to his feet, he heard terrible screams coming from Martha inside the house. There were also the snarls and growls of some unfathomable beast. Suddenly all went silent and von Breber crept towards the door, drawing his sword. He threw his body against it, knocking it from its hinges and fell into a room he would rather not have seen. Pieces of human flesh were littered across it and piled in its corners. What remained of poor Martha lay on the floor and crouched over her was a huge werewolf, which, although it

The Burgomeister

In Bavaria, in the town of Ansbach, in 1685, a wolf was terrorizing the inhabitants and had savaged and killed a number of women and children as well as many animals. A rumour began to spread that the wolf was in fact the town's late Burgomeister, or mayor, a hated figure who had recently died. Hunters set out to search for the beast and eventually cornered it, chasing it into a well where it drowned.

They pulled the creature's body from the well and dressed it in the clothing of the late Burgomeister, even putting a false beard on it and a mask resembling his face. They hung it from a gibbet and after a while, cut it down and put it in the town's museum to remind everyone that werewolves do exist.

It is said that the last-ever killing of a werewolf took place in the town of Wittlich in Germany's Rhineland-Palatinate region.

A German werewolf kills two children and makes off with a third in his jaws, while their mother cries for help. By Lucas Cranach the Elder (1472-1553).

had the beautiful body of a woman and long blond hair, the head, blood-covered hands and feet were those of a wolf.

It looked up at the Count and let out a loud growl before turning to make good its escape, but he lunged forward, driving the blade deep into the werewolf's back, right up to the hilt. The Count was stunned for a moment as the figure before him began to change. Gradually, he realized that it was changing before him into the woman to whom he had devoted his life, his beloved wife, Hilda. The building he was in was actually the summerhouse of his own property but he had failed to recognize it in the darkness. He thought back to her scooping that handful of water from a shimmering stream in the Hartz Mountains and the story told by the innkeeper that he had, sadly, not believed at the time.

WOLF ROCK

The great storytellers, the Brothers Grimm, were told a story around 1817 about how a rocky cliff known as Wolf Rock in a meadow overlooking Seehausen, near the village of Eggensted in the Magdeburg region was given its name.

It was said that a long time ago, a stranger had settled in the Brandsleber Forest close to Eggensted. Nobody knew his real name and he was consequently known simply as 'The Old Man'. He worked as a labourer and sometimes a shepherd and one day he was taken on by a farmer to shear a flock of sheep. At the end of the day when the owner arrived to check on The Old Man's progress, the sheep were fine, but there was no sign of either The Old Man or one particularly distinctive spotted lamb.

The Legend of Wolf Rock

He was absent for a long time but one day, as the farmer tended his flock, The Old Man suddenly re-appeared and told him sarcastically that his spotted lamb sent his greetings. The other man was furious and launched himself at The Old Man who suddenly turned into a wolf in front of his eyes and attacked him. The farmer's sheepdogs ran to their master's protection, rounding on the wolf and chasing it through the woods. Eventually, they cornered it at the edge of a cliff, but it changed back into the human form of The Old Man and began to beg for mercy. The farmer was not listening to the fiend, however. He drove his dogs at him and forced The Old Man off the cliff to his death a long way below. The cliff is known as Wolf Rock to this day.

THE LAST WEREWOLF

In 1812, following Napoleon Bonaparte's defeat at Moscow, there were mass desertions from his army. One man, Thomas Johannes Baptist Schwytzer, travelling home in the company of a number of other deserters, noticed a farm as he passed close to Wittlich. By this time, the men were starving. They decided to rob the farm of whatever food they could find. As they began to look around the outhouses, they were interrupted by the farmer and his sons. In the ensuing struggle, the farmer and his sons were murdered. They had been seen by the farmer's wife and Schwytzer decided that she, too, would have to die. As he was about to finish her off she screamed a curse at him, telling him that from that day forward, every time there was a full moon, he would turn into a rabid wolf.

Horrific Transformation

The curse worked and with every full moon, Schwytzer would undergo a horrific transformation, becoming savage and violently robbing homes and businesses, raping women and girls and killing anyone who got in his way whilst the madness was on him. Eventually, he was abandoned by everyone and was left to roam the forests and hills alone. One day, his crimes caught up with him, however, after he raped a farmer's daughter. The inhabitants of the village in which she lived hunted him down to a spot close to the village of Morbach and killed him.

Superstitious Beliefs

He was buried at a crossroads and above his grave was built a shrine in which a candle burned. If the candle was ever allowed to go out, the superstitious villagers declared, the werewolf would return. The story does not end there, however, because it has been reported that in 1988, a group of American servicemen, based at Morbach, were driving past the shrine when they noticed that the candle had been extinguished. They laughed about the notion of a werewolf being on the loose. Later that night, the alarms at the base went off, indicating that something was interfering with the perimeter fence. A guard who went to investigate reported seeing a huge creature that looked like a dog standing on its hind legs, staring straight at him. Later when they brought a guard dog to the area where the creature had been seen, it cowered and whimpered in terror. Needless to say, the candle at the shrine was immediately re-lit.

Woodcut of 1669 from edition of Gesner Historiae animalum depicting a forest demon said to have inhabited forests near Salzburg and Hamburg, Germany.

SCANDINAVIA

Scandinavian werewolf lore probably has its origins in the habit that Norse warriors had of dressing themselves in the skins of beasts they had killed. By doing so, they believed that they seemed even more ferocious to their enemies.

Wolf costumes are mentioned in the Sagas, the stories about ancient Scandinavian and Germanic history that have been passed down through generations. Often they have no supernatural qualities whatsoever. However, it is easy to see how the supernatural could be attached to figures such as the *berserker*, the warriors who people lived in fear of encountering. The law was that any man challenged to a fight would automatically forfeit his lands and his wife if he failed to accept the challenge. Of course, if they accepted the challenge, they were highly unlikely to be able to defeat the ferocious fighting machine that was a *berserker*. They, therefore, travelled the land challenging farmers and claiming swathes of land and numerous women. Through time, it is understandable that the magical powers of trolls or *jötunns* (superhumanly strong nature spirits) were attributed to them. It is undeniable, however, that an incident of *berserker* rage could seem to be invested with diabolical possession. They are reported to have assumed incredible strength at these moments and seemed almost invulnerable to pain. They foamed at the mouth and are said to have gnawed at the rims of their shields as they waited to do battle. Moreover, when they attacked they howled like wolves.

The Sagas contain numerous references to shapeshifting and different methods of achieving it. The *Ynglinga Saga* describes how, 'Odin could transform his shape: his body would lie as if dead, or asleep; but then he would be in shape of a fish, or worm, or bird, or beast, and be off in a twinkling to distant lands upon his own or other people's business.'

Danish king Harold sent a warlock to Iceland in the shape of a whale, leaving his body in a cataleptic state at home. The *Saga of Hrolf Krake* tells of the hero Bödvar Bjarki fighting in the shape of a huge bear while his body lies comatose, as if drunk. The *Vatnsdaela Saga* talks of three Finns who were ordered by a Norwegian chieftain to go to Finland and report back on the state of the country because he was interested in settling there. Their bodies became rigid and only their souls went on the errand. After three days, they provided the information that had been requested although the saga does not tell whether they achieved this by transmigrating into the souls of birds or animals. The third method was to change only in the eyes of the beholder which would have been bewitched.

Rampant Werewolves

Bishop Olaf Magnussen, writing as Olaus Magnus in the 16th century, stated that the livestock of the people who lived in Prussia, Lithuania, and Livonia was often lost to bands of wolves. Worse still, however, according to Olaus Magnus, was the loss to werewolves. He claimed that large numbers of werewolves roamed those regions, and their victims included not only animals, but also humans. They attacked remote farms and broke into people's homes, savaging every living thing that stood in their way. According to him, Livonian werewolves were initiated by drinking a cup of specially brewed beer and reciting a particular spell. Their favourite meeting place was at an old castle near Courland, in present-day western Latvia, a frightening place that people avoided. But even werewolves were in some danger when they went there, because the strongest amongst them had no compunction about killing the weaker ones. Elliot O'Donnell says in his 1912 book, *Werewolves*, that 'at one time, werewolves were to be met with almost daily in Denmark.' In Sweden, a country with a long and savage werewolf radition, there are old women, known as *Vargamors*, who are associated with packs of wolves, often securing human victims for them.

LISO OF SOAROA

She was a beautiful, but vain and spoilt woman, mother of three children: a girl and two boys. One day, she received an invitation from an aunt who lived in Skatea, asking her to come and visit with her children. As the aunt was very well off and Liso was her nearest living relative, she thought it politic to accept the invitation.

Thrown to the Wolves

She set off with her children, driving a sledge pulled by one horse through a dark forest. The horse suddenly panicked when it was set upon by a pack of snarling and obviously hungry wolves. Of course, if the wolves brought the horse to ground, her own life and those of her children would be in grave danger but she suddenly came up with an idea. It was regrettable, but it was all she could think of. She would sacrifice her children one at a time to the wolves. Hopefully, by the time she had thrown the third from the carriage, she would be near to habitation. So, one by one, her children were thrown screaming from the carriage and torn to pieces by the wolves.

Shortly after she had thrown the third one from the sledge, she came to a house where she pulled up the terrified horse. An old hag confronted her at the door and ushered her into the house, just before the wolves arrived and pressed their cold, wet noses against the window. The old woman smiled and told Liso that all she had to do was open the door and they would rush in and devour her as they had her children. But, Liso said, they would also eat you, surely? The old woman laughed and told Liso with a wicked sneer on her lips that they could not as she was a *vargamor* that the wolves loved like a mother.

Intense Fear

Liso was beside herself with fear and swore that she would do anything the old lady wanted, as long as she did not let the wolves in. The hag thought for a moment and then replied that she would spare Liso, but only if she would remain with her forever and do all the housework that she was now too old to do. And so, Liso set to work, spending every waking minute being ordered around

by the old hag. Still, however, the wolves gathered outside, howling and scratching at the windows until eventually the old woman declared that she could keep them at bay no longer. Liso would have to be fed to them.

Liso collapsed to her knees, pleading for her life with such passion that the old woman eventually said that she would indeed spare her but only if she found someone to take her place. She told her to write a note to someone and ask them to come. She would see to it that it was delivered. Liso sat down and wrote to her husband, Oscar, telling him that she had had an accident and asking him to come and fetch her. Several days later, Oscar's carriage arrived outside the house and Liso called to him from her room. As she did so, a realization fell upon her, firstly of what she had done to her children and secondly how much love she had for her husband. It gave her renewed strength and as the *vargamor* shuffled across the room to summon her wolves, Liso threw herself at the old woman and struck her on the head with a heavy ornament. Then she ran outside, seized her husband by the arm and pushed him into the carriage. The coachman whipped the horses and they sped off into the night with the wolves in hot, snarling pursuit. As they gained on the carriage, Liso wondered about a sacrifice. The coachman was nothing but a poor, uneducated man; he would not be missed. But then, as she realized her husband, a good man, would never agree to her idea, it struck her that the coachman had a wife and children who loved him and depended on him. She suddenly knew that she had sacrificed all of that to save her own life. She decided to offer her life as a sacrifice and perhaps to atone for her dreadful, cowardly acts.

Disgust

But her husband would not agree to it, insisting that the two horses would outrun the pack of wolves. And sure enough, they gradually began to outdistance them and soon left them far behind. At last Liso was able to explain to Oscar what had happened to their children. He was understandably shocked and calling her a murderess, he denounced her as even worse than the *vargamor* she had killed. He stopped the coach, climbed out and ordered the coachman to drive her back to her parents home. He wanted nothing more to do with her. As the carriage started on its journey, she stared blankly out of the window, her heart full of love for the first time in her life, but destined to forever be distanced from it.

PORTUGAL

The writer, John Latouche wrote *Travels in Portugal* in 1875, describing his journeys in that part of the world. The following story was told to him by a man one night over a glass of wine.

When he was younger, the man had worked, along with a few other labourers, for a farmer who had newly acquired his farm. The farmer's wife was pregnant and the couple decided they needed another woman around the place to do the work she would shortly be unable to do. The narrator of the story was to be dispatched to the nearest town, Ponte de Lima, to try to find a suitable woman.

He set out the next morning but had only travelled a mile when he came across a girl sitting at the side of the road. 'One of the queerest looking girls my eyes ever fell on', was how he described her, wrapped up in a brown cloak of a type not worn in that part of Portugal. She was stretching out her hands to catch the rays of the sun. The reason she looked so odd, he said, was because her hair was cropped close to her head, like a man's. He had never seen a young girl like her.

They talked and she told him she had come from Tarouca which was quite a long way away. She was named Joana and was in search of work as a servant. The man was delighted. She was just what he was looking for and she would save him the long journey to Ponte de Lima. He told her that he was looking for just such a person and invited her back to the farm. She was engaged and, not long after, when the baby was born, she took the place of the mistress of the house.

A Bewitched Baby

The new baby was healthy but an old woman who lived nearby and was thought to be a 'wise woman', declared that she believed it to be bewitched. The new parents laughed but the old woman said she would not be surprised if the devil's mark was not on its skin somewhere. They examined their child and to their horror, there it was. A small crescent or half-moon had been pricked on the baby's skin with a pin or another sharp object. Everyone was immediately afraid but the old woman told them they need only be afraid at the time of the new moon. At that time the child must be watched all night. She left the house, passing the servant girl wrapped in her brown cloak, pretending to be asleep.

Terrible Temper

Time passed and life continued as normal. The servant girl worked hard, but occasionally displayed a terrible temper. The remainder of the time, however, she was pleasant enough. One day she was in conversation with her master and mistress and she confessed that she knew what the mark on the child signified. Children with that mark, she told them, grow into *lobis-homems*, or werewolves, before they reach the age of 16, unless something is done to prevent it happening.

Desperate Measures

When they asked how they could prevent it, she told them that the mark had to be covered with the blood of a white pigeon and the child must be left naked on a blanket on the mountainside the first time the new moon rises. The moon, she told them, will draw up the mark through the pigeon's blood and the child will be saved from its terrible fate. They agreed to do it and a day or two later, the child was laid on the mountainside near the house just before the new moon rose. It was essential, the girl told them, that no eye should fall on the child until the moon had risen. The farmer was, naturally, nervous, worrying that the child might be savaged by a wolf, but the other men on the farm who knew the local region, assured him that no

wolves had been seen in this area for many years. He loaded his gun regardless, filling it with rusty nails in the absence of ammunition. As he did so there were the most chilling screams from the location where the child had been placed. Everyone rushed from the house to the child's aid, as the screams increased in volume. As they neared the spot, they were horrified to see a huge brown wolf looming over the body of the child, blood dripping from his fangs and his eyes glowing orange like fire.

Joana's True Identity

The wolf made to escape as they approached and the farmer opened fire. The wolf fell to the ground and he was struck with a heavy piece of wood. The wolf, however, managed to clamber to his feet and limped off into the cover of the surrounding darkness. Sadly, the child was dead, its throat ripped open by the wolf's fangs and the blanket drenched in its blood. Suddenly, it struck them that Joana had not been seen since the child had been placed out there on the mountainside. It dawned on them that she was, in fact, a *lobis-homem* and had murdered the baby. The next morning, they returned to the mountainside and followed the trail of the wounded wolf. Not far into the woods, they found her, stretched out on the ground, in her human form, covered in blood. Through her pain, she tried to explain that she had crept into the woods after they had left the child, in order to watch over it but had been attacked by the wolf. When the gun fired, she had been hit and had been there ever since. They went for the priest, but she was dead by the time he arrived. The farmer noticed before they buried her that she had a mark on her arm exactly where he had struck the wolf.

RUSSIA AND EASTERN EUROPE

Sixteenth-century writer, Bishop Olaus Magnus, noted in 1555 that although much livestock was lost to wolves, it was nothing compared to the loss of men to werewolves. Magnus believed that werewolves would congregate in one particular area, a place so frightening that humans were too terrified to visit.

'In Prussia, Livonia, and Lithuania, although the inhabitants suffer considerably from the rapacity of wolves throughout the year, in that these animals rend their cattle, which are scattered in great numbers through the woods, whenever they stray in the very least, yet this is not regarded by them as such a serious matter as what they endure from men turned into wolves.

On the feast of the Nativity of Christ, at night, such a multitude of wolves transformed from men gather together in a certain spot, arranged among themselves, and then spread to rage with wondrous ferocity against human beings, and those animals which are not wild, that the natives of these regions suffer more detriment from these, than they do from true and natural wolves; for when a human habitation has been detected by them isolated in the woods, they besiege it with atrocity, striving to break in the doors, and in the event of their doing so, they devour all the human beings, and every animal which is found within. They burst into the beer-cellars, and there they empty the tuns of beer or mead, and pile up the empty casks one above another in the middle of the cellar, thus showing their difference from natural and genuine wolves...

Between Lithuania, Livonia, and Courland are the walls of a certain old ruined castle. At this spot congregate thousands, on a fixed occasion, and try their agility in jumping. Those who are unable to bound over the wall, as is often the case with the fattest, are fallen upon with scourges by the captains and slain.

Bishop Magnus, 1555.

RUSSIA

Russia was made for the werewolf, known to the inhabitants as *oborot*, 'one transformed'. Huge, grey, cold and filled with vast uncultivated territories, often densely forested, its underpopulated wastes are a breeding ground for lycanthropy.

Lycanthropic flowers are in abundance, in several different varieties. Apart from the normal white and yellow werewolf flowers, there is said to be a red species and one that is of a bluish tinge which is said to glow in the dark. There are also orange lycanthropic flowers that are covered in black spots and grow in damp, fetid places. The werewolf

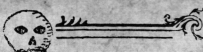
can also be found on Russia's plains, on the arid wastes at the foot of the Urals, the Caucasus and other mountains, as well as on the tundras that hug the shore of the Arctic Ocean. Its favourite haunts, however, are the Caucasus and Ural Mountains, areas that have traditionally been imbued with an air of mystery and which have had associations with the supernatural through the centuries. It was in a village in the Ural Mountains that the devil is reputed to have changed six men into wolves for not paying homage to him.

Female Werewolves

But, in Russia, it is not only men who become werewolves. Women too can be transformed. It is said that women want to be werewolves more than men, women having acquired the power by their own acts not by heredity. For women, it is also said, the metamorphosis into wolf is desired in order to wreak revenge on another person, whether it be an unfaithful husband, lover or another woman. It is also said that when women are in their werewolf state, they are more savage than their male counterparts, as well as more daring.

IVAN AND BREDA THE WEREWOLF

There was once a man named Ivan who lived in the village of Shiganska, a small settlement on the left bank of the Petchora. It was an area where lycanthropic blue and white flowers could be found and people wishing to become werewolves travelled there from all over in order to find the means of their transformation. The woods were filled not just with werewolves, but also with all sorts of otherworldly creatures.

Ivan was a hunter who was doing very well for himself. He lived with his mother and two sisters. One day he set out for a day's hunting with his beloved dog Dolk. Finding the tracks of a deer, he set his dog loose and began to stalk the animal. Eventually, he spied it and tried to get within shooting range. Suddenly, however, the barking of his dog ahead changed to a yelping howl of pain. Ivan forgot the deer and ran forward seeing ahead of him two dark objects on the snow. It was Dolk and he had been bitten in half by a wolf that had run off as Ivan approached.

Ivan meets Breda

Ivan was distraught, having reared the dog from a puppy. Finding the wolf's tracks, he resolved to hunt it down and take revenge. He followed them to a dark cavern in the side of a hill and was wondering what to do next when he heard a peal of laughter echoing off the walls inside the cavern. Suddenly, standing in front of him was a beautiful girl, the most beautiful, in fact, that he had ever seen. She was dressed head to foot in white fur and told him her name was Breda. She told him she lived there with her father, a recluse, and that he had better go before her father discovered him there, because he detested other people. Ivan, however, refused to leave the girl and eventually only said farewell as the sun was beginning to set.

Suspicions Start to Grow

He returned, however, and courted the girl until finally she agreed to marry him. She came to live with him and his mother and sisters but they found her cold and unfriendly and did not take to her.

Soon after, neighbours began to com-

plain that they were losing livestock and speculated that there must be a wolf in the neighbourhood. In fact, they said, when they followed the creature's tracks, they ended under the walls of Ivan's house. Ivan said he had heard nothing as did the other members of his family, but people began to look oddly at Breda. Eventually, they refused to speak to her. One night when the weather was very bad, Ivan was unable to sleep. As he lay awake, he heard the door of his wife's room open quietly, followed by light steps along the passage. There was a muffled cry and then silence again. Ivan got up to find its source but Breda called to him to go back to bed. She told him she had been feeling unwell. He did as she told him.

The following morning, Ivan's older sister, Beata, was found dead in her bed. Her throat, breast and stomach were split open, her flesh savaged and eaten. A week later, his other sister, Malvina, met the same fate and Ivan's mother angrily told him that he must be under a spell of some kind, because a normal man would go out and avenge himself on the creature that had killed his sisters. Filled with guilt, during that night and many after, Ivan stayed up, a gun at his side. One night, he had just fallen asleep when he heard loud screams for help. Seeing a huge white wolf in the house, he opened fire and ran to his mother's bedside. He was too late, however. She was already dead.

On the Murderer's Trail

He followed a track of blood from the room that led directly to his wife's door. Inside, he found Breda on the floor, wounded in the shoulder, undoubtedly by a bullet from his gun. She opened her eyes and he melted with gratitude that she was still alive. She explained that yes, she was a werewolf, but that she was a werewolf by choice. She had eaten a lycanthropic flower so she would be transformed into a werewolf in order to take revenge on her former husband who had treated her badly. She begged him to clean up all signs of what had occurred that night and to protect her from the villagers. Ivan did as he was asked, telling neighbours that his mother had died suddenly of heart failure. The neighbours were still curious, however, and Ivan spent his life in a state of anxiety in case the truth was discovered. Some time passed, but the secret wore Ivan down until he could stand it no more. He sought the advice of a local old man who was believed to be very wise. The old man told him that he would need to have his wife exorcised. Otherwise, she would eventually be found out and hunted to a horrific end by the people of the village.

Albertus Pericofcius

Albertus Pericofcius tyrannized and harassed his subjects unscrupulously. One night when he was away from home, his herd of cattle, which he had acquired by extortion, perished. On his return, when he was told of his loss, he was furious and started blaspheming, exclaiming, 'Let him who has slain, eat; if God chooses, let him devour me as well.'

As he spoke, drops of blood fell to earth and the nobleman was suddenly transformed into a wild dog. He rushed amongst his dead cattle, tore and savaged the carcasses and began to eat them. His wife, who was pregnant, died of fear.

A Surprise Exorcism

He told Breda what the old man had recommended, but she was furious that he even dared to mention exorcism. Undeterred, Ivan decided to do it anyway. He would catch her when she was least expecting it. One evening when the moon was full and she had just transformed into her lupine form, he crept into her room with the old man and two assistants. A desperate struggle ensued, but eventually they overpowered her and tied her up. They carried her to the back of the house where they placed her in the middle of an equilateral red triangle that had been chalked on the ground. Seven or eight feet west of the triangle, they lit a fire over which they hung a pot containing a mixture of hypericum, vinegar, sulphur, cayenne, and mountain ash berries.

The old man knelt down, crossed himself on the forehead and chest and prayed until the mixture in the pot began to emit strong fumes. He then stood up and he and the two assistants approached the wolf with switches cut from a mountain ash, ready to flog her. But Ivan could not bear to see the woman he loved flogged before his eyes. He ran at the men, grabbed the switches and sent them packing. He knelt beside his wife, the werewolf, and undid her bonds. She stood up, a huge white wolf, stared for a moment into his eyes and with a look, more human than animal, ran off into the darkness never to be seen again.

POLAND

In Poland, werewolves are said to roam twice a year - at Christmas and mid-summer. One Polish tale suggests that if a girdle of human skin is laid across the threshold of a house in which a marriage is being celebrated, the entire marriage party will be transformed into werewolves if they step across it. After three years they will recover their natural form, the story goes on, if the witch who enchanted them in the first place covers them with skins with the hair turned outwards. Another story says that on one occasion a witch used a skin that failed to cover the entire body of a bridegroom who had been enchanted in this way and, although he resumed his human form, he was left with the tail of a wolf.

Antonio de Torquemada

Spanish writer, Antonio de Torquemada, in his book *Jardin de las Flores Curiosas*, written in 1570, wrote about a warlock who was also a werewolf. The creature had become infamous in Russia and a Russian prince had resolved to kill him. He sent out his soldiers with orders to catch the warlock and bring him before him. They succeeded and before too long the monster was standing in front of him in chains. The prince was keen to see the transformation from human to wolf and he managed to trick the warlock into demonstrating it to him. The warlock reluctantly agreed, adjourned to a neighbouring room and came out, a growling, snarling wolf. The devious prince was prepared. He had two hungry dogs ready and unleashed them on the wolf which was ripped to shreds within minutes.

Scene still from *An American Werewolf in Paris*,
Anthony Waller, 1997.

NATIVE AMERICAN WEREWOLVES

The wolf has long been an animal of sacred importance to many Native American tribes, featuring in numerous legends, and celebrated in ritual and song. It is seen in a very different light to the 'big bad wolf' so prevalent in European tales. In Native American myth the wolf is almost always revered as wise and powerful rather than threatening and sinister. To some tribes, notably the Shoshone and Arikara, the wolf is a creator spirit, responsible for bringing humankind into existence. Others tell of the wolf saving men, and teaching them the skills they need to survive.

COYOTE

Alongside the wolf often runs the coyote, frequently portrayed as the wolf's mischievous younger brother. The coyote is a 'trickster' spirit who uses guile and deceit to achieve his aim - which is often to expose the fallibility of humankind. As with many Native American spirits, he has the ability to shapeshift into any form he chooses. This deep seated belief in shapeshifters, married with an ancient reverence for the wolf, makes Native American legends a fertile hunting ground for those who have a fascination with werewolves.

SKINWALKERS

Many Native American tribes share a belief in malevolent witches who can change shape at will. These 'skinwalkers' feature most prominently in the legends of the tribes of the south-west, and are particularly associated with the Navajo, who term them *Yee naaldooshi* (or 'they that walk on all fours'). Though the nature of the Skinwalker varies from one account to the next, there are a couple of things that all the tribes seem to agree on. Firstly, Skinwalkers usually dress in wolf or coyote skins, making them look a lot like werewolves (they are sometimes referred to as 'Navajo Wolves'). And secondly, running into a Skinwalker is incredibly bad news.

Even talking about Skinwalkers is considered dangerous, which is one of the reasons why specific information about them is so scarce. For the Navajo, witchcraft (or *adishgash*) is a very real part of their everyday lives, and many refuse to have their photographs taken in case the picture is used to cause them harm through 'sympathetic magic'. They

believe that speaking something aloud can cause it to happen. As the most feared witch of them all is the Skinwalker, and the Navajo live on the paths of these Skinwalkers, it is hardly surprising there is a reluctance to talk about them to outsiders.

Legend has it that to become a Skinwalker, a witch must first kill a blood relative with sorcery, and then eat the corpse's flesh. After this, the witch obtains the power to change into any animal they wish, and they acquire the strength, speed and killing power of whichever animal they choose to become. They are considered greedy, selfish and duplicitous, committing acts of malice purely for malice's sake. During the day, the Skinwalker can look like any other person, except that their eyes reflect light like a wolf's. At night their eyes reflect no light, which is one way to tell them apart from wild animals.

Corpse Powder

Some say that their eyes glow red or yellow at night, and if their gaze meets yours then they are obliged to kill you. Death might come in any number of ways - Skinwalkers are able to curse their victims, take control of their victims in order to force them to kill themselves, or simply tear their victims to shreds with wolf-like claws. In addition they are believed to carry corpse powder - made from the ground-down bones of the dead. If this powder is blown into a victim's face, he or she will suffer agonizing convulsions before dropping dead. The good news for those who do not have Navajo blood is that Skinwalkers are believed to only attack the Navajo themselves. Nonetheless, there have been persistent reports of close encounters with ferocious beast-men prowling at night on land that once belonged to Native Americans. If these creatures of the night really are Skinwalkers, it seems nobody has

Scene still from *Skinwalkers*, James Isaac, 2006.

told them which humans they can and cannot attack.

There are clear parallels between claimed sightings of Skinwalkers and alleged encounters with the other famous North American wild-man creature, the Sasquatch or 'Bigfoot'. Indeed many believe the Sasquatch is itself a Skinwalker, taking the form of an ape or bear. Some have gone so far as to suggest that other paranormal activity might also be the work of these shapeshifting witches, and Skinwalkers transforming into birds or bats have even been offered as an explanation for sightings of unidentified flying objects.

Chindi

The Navajo believe a Chindi is released when a person takes their dying breath. Akin to a ghost, it is a spirit that represents everything that was bad about the person who has passed away. This malign force is believed to be able to cause sickness and death in others. The Navajo often attempt to ensure a death occurs outdoors in order to allow the Chindi to disperse, sometimes burning the deceased's possessions to try and ensure that the Chindi has nothing to inhabit or infect. If a death occurs in a home, the home is often abandoned.

Think you've seen a werewolf? Take a closer look, and it may turn out to be a Chindi. Some reports suggest that a Chindi can inhabit the body of an animal, and one form it might choose is a passing wolf or coyote. As with so many Native American beliefs, details about the Chindi are hard to pin down because few people who truly believe in them wish to speak about them aloud. To do so is thought to invite unwelcome attention from the Chindi. If you do suspect you are facing a Chindi, however, you might try drawing a circle around you - some reports suggest that may keep you safe. Certainly a silver bullet will be of no use to you - the Chindi is a spirit and thus impervious to any weapons.

WOLF LEGENDS OF THE QUILEUTE TRIBE

The Quileute tribe were catapulted from relative obscurity to international stardom by the vampire-based book and film franchise *Twilight*, which portrayed them as lycanthropic shapeshifters who are the arch enemies of the vampires. The writer of the original books, Stephenie Meyer, developed a legend about the tribe which has since passed into the realm of urban myth. In her story, the Quileute can transform themselves into werewolves to attack vampires. The lead Quileute character in the book, Jacob Black, has become a cult hero, and interest in the Quileute has exploded as a result. Although there is no such shapeshifting legend in Quileute culture itself, it is true that the Quileute have a special affinity with wolves, and believe their ancestors were originally transformed from wolves into human beings.

The Quileute creation myth tells that the great Native American transformer Q'wati (sometimes known as *Dokibatt*) came to their lands and found no people living there. He first placed his hands into a lake, and rubbed them together, until the dead skin between his palms formed a small ball. He released this ball into the lake and turned it into fish, so that humans would have something to eat. He then saw two wolves, and transformed them into human beings - the first Quileute people. He gave the tribe its name, and told them that they would always be brave and strong, because they came from wolves. And because he saw that the wolves always travelled in pairs, one male and one female, he decreed that the Quileute men would only take one wife each (though this rule did not apply to Chiefs).

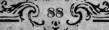

Q'wati also taught the Quileute how to hunt and fish, and he features in the creation myths of several other Native American tribes too, always as a protector and friend to humankind. The Quileute honour him, and their ancestors, by enacting a 'wolf dance', which involves wearing a wolf mask carved from cedar wood. Ceremonies featuring the wolf dance continue to be performed on their one square mile reservation at La Push, Washington (on the Pacific coast) to this day. Preserving the tradition is especially important to the Quileute, since they believe that their only brothers, the Chimakum tribe, were washed away by a flood. They thus represent the last of their wolf-born kind.

Though their traditional industry has always been fishing, in recent years the Quileute have turned to tourism to try and generate income - much of it coming from fans of the *Twilight* series, who visit the reservation from all over the world to try and discover the truth behind the shapeshifting wolves that Meyer created. The real legends of the Quileute speak of an ogress who eats children, and a giant wild man who catches fish with his razor-sharp toenails, but the only shapeshifter they believe in is the trickster figure of the Raven - and his stories are usually comic rather than terrifying. Nonetheless, the ancient story that the tribe was created from wolves, melded with the modern tale that the Quileute might have the power to change back into that form, has proved to be one that has captured the popular imagination. The Quileute have found a way to use this modern day myth to ensure their own ancient beliefs are preserved for future generations.

SKIDI PAWNEE

The Skidi Pawnee are so closely associated with wolves that they are sometimes called the 'Wolf Pawnee'. An important Pawnee creation myth states that a council of all the animals was once held in the sky, but the Wolf Star was not invited. Resenting this, the Wolf Star sent down a grey wolf to follow The Storm That Comes From The West, who had been charged with looking after all the life on earth. The Storm carried with him a bag which contained all of the world's human beings. Whenever he found a good spot for buffalo hunting, he would release the people from the bag.

Mindless Rage

The wolf waited until The Storm was sleeping, and then stole the bag, thinking it might contain food. When the wolf opened the bag all the human beings rushed out, and when they realized there were no buffalo to hunt they became angry with the wolf. In a mindless rage they killed him. In due course The Storm found them, and saw what they had done. He told them that they had now brought death into the world for the first time, and it would stay with them forever. He instructed them to make a bag from the wolf's skin, and fill it with things that would remind them of the terrible deed they had done. From now on, The Storm told them, they would be known as the Skidi, or Wolf Pawnee.

To the early settlers, the Skidi Pawnee were a notoriously war-like tribe who defended their sacred lands tenaciously. They associated constellations of stars with animals, and held ceremonies to ensure the spirits were pleased. One of their most notorious ceremonies was the 'Morning Star Ceremony', in the course of which a young

girl was ritually sacrificed. This ceremony occurred whenever a member of the tribe had a dream that the Morning Star required a sacrifice. The tribe would then capture a young girl from a neighbouring tribe in order to sacrifice her by firing arrows into her heart. The last sacrifice occurred in 1848, when a girl called Haxti, aged 14, was the unfortunate victim.

THE WENDIGO

Although it has recently become closely associated with the legend of the werewolf, the Wendigo (sometimes spelt *Windigo*) of Native American legend is quite a different creature, more accurately described as a shapeshifter. The Algonquian tribes believe that human beings can be 'possessed' by the Wendigo, with those who engage in cannibalism being especially likely to become victims. Indeed some variants of the legend say that human beings are transformed into Wendigos simply by eating human flesh, rather than becoming possessed by a spirit. Other versions suggest that intense greed is enough to turn a human into a Wendigo. The transformation generally occurs in winter, with many accounts stating that a Wendigo can shapeshift back into a human in the spring.

Desire for Human Flesh

However and whenever the transformation occurs, the resulting half-human creature is always said to be violent and gluttonous, with an insatiable desire for human flesh. The Wendigo looks like a recently disinterred human corpse, emaciated, bloody and part-decomposed, with an ash-grey complexion and a strong odour of decaying

flesh. The Wendigo's appetite for human beings can never be satisfied, as every time it feeds it grows larger, thus requiring ever more food to sustain itself. It is therefore always ravenously hungry, and close to starvation, no matter how often it eats. To kill a Wendigo and stop its feeding frenzy, you must burn its body and scatter the ashes.

The confusion between the Wendigo and werewolves seems to stem from a number of reported sightings of wolf-like creatures in the North American states of Wisconsin and Michigan, broadly the same area as the Wendigo is said to inhabit. The 'Bray Road Beast' and 'Michigan Dogman' are both said to be wolf-like in appearance, but with human characteristics such as walking on two legs. It is perhaps unsurprising that sightings of werewolf-like creatures have become linked to ancient tales of malevolent spirits in the same area, but in truth the Wendigo is much closer in appearance and behaviour to a zombie than it is to a werewolf.

THE NAGUAL

The Nagual (sometimes *Nahual*) of Mexico is a sorcerer who has a special affinity with an 'animal spirit' (or *Tonal*). The legend appears to predate the arrival of Europeans, and so would seem to be quite distinct from the medieval European tales of werewolves. The Nagual and his (or her) animal companion are spiritually linked throughout their lives, living and dying together. At night the human can transform himself into its animal companion form, so that in effect the two become one. Any wound inflicted on the animal whilst it is being controlled by the Nagual will show on the human body of the Nagual when he changes back, for example.

The link between a human and a particular animal was established at birth, depending on the day that the person was born. Persons born on a day representing the wolf, for example, might have a special affinity with wolves. The most common forms chosen by Naguals are owls, bats, jaguars and pumas - but in theory a Nagual can shapeshift into any animal form.

Many stories talk of the Nagual feeding on sleeping children, and some Mexican parents hang mirrors above their children's beds for this reason - the reflection of the child is said to ward off the Nagual. There are other tales that talk of the Nagual sucking blood and causing disease. Others suggest that the Nagual cannot directly harm a human being, and the Nagual appears to have been an accepted member of some societies. They were tolerated and fed by the host society in order to protect against other malign spirits or more hostile Naguals.

A North American Indian shaman wearing wolf skin with tambourine and spear, from *Illustrations of the Manners, Customs and Condition of the North American Indians*, George Catlin, 1876.

THE IJIRAAT

This Inuit shapeshifting creature can take any form, but most frequently adopts the guise of a wolf, with only its glowing red eyes betraying its true nature. Often those who claim to have seen Ijiraat state that they did so from the corner of their eye, fleetingly, as the Ijiraat seemed to vanish into thin air. The Ijiraat favour forms that are adept at moving swiftly through the Arctic landscape, which may be why they are so often sighted as wolves. Ravens and bears are the amongst the other commonly reported forms.

Opinions differ as to how dangerous the Ijiraat might be to humans - some say they attack frequently, especially children, but others maintain they are simply messengers or 'lost souls'. In one version of the story, the Ijiraat are said to be Inuit people who travelled too far North, and found themselves trapped between the land of the living and the land of the dead. One thing that all accounts seem to agree upon is that anyone who encounters the Ijiraat will quickly lose all memory of the event.

QISARUATSIAQ

Qisaruatsiaq was an Inuit woman who, according to legend, left her community and as a result was transformed into a wolf. Qisaruatisaq is described as a stubborn loner, who insisted on building her own ice house rather than sharing with the rest of the community. She would go fishing alone, and often return empty-handed, whereupon she would steal from her neighbours. One day, Qiasaruatsiaq did not return from one of her lonely fishing trips, and so a tracker set off to find her. Following her snowy footprints

deep inland he journeyed for many miles, until he noticed that one of her footprints had turned into the imprint of a wolf's claw. The half-human half-wolf tracks disappeared into the distance, and the tracker decided it was wiser for him to turn back.

After this, many locals reported seeing Qisaruatsiaq in her new wolf form when they were out hunting caribou. They believe that she grew wilder and wilder until she finally transformed into a pure wolf. In Greenland there is a similar legend, that of the Qivittoq, described as a wandering spirit who, having left his community, grows claws and fur until he becomes more animal than human. The Qivittoq is said to sometimes return to the community in order to steal food.

THE AMAROK

The Amarok is said to be a giant wolf-like creature of the Arctic, that always hunts alone. Some have suggested that the legend of the Amarok may date back to a time when giant wolves did indeed live alongside mankind, with the now extinct dire wolf being cited as one possible explanation for the story. The dire wolf was considerably larger than the modern day grey wolf and would have been known to the Inuit's distant ancestors, dying out around 10,000 years ago. There is no suggestion of any human-like behaviour from the Amarok, it is simply reported to be a ferocious wolf-like creature which is around the size of a fully grown man.

The description of the Amarok has close parallels with another mythical giant wolf, the Waheela. This is said to dwell in the Northwest territories of Canada, and to hunt in small packs of twos or threes.

HOUNDS OF GOD

Werewolves are generally seen as agents of evil, often in league with the devil in their terrorizing of innocent citizens. Sometimes it is said that people are transformed against their will. These people were given the binomial name *melancholia canina* in the 10th century and in the 14th century, they were called *daemonium lupum*.

In 1692, in the town of Jurgensberg in Livonia, an old man claimed that werewolves were not evil. He himself claimed to be one, a highly dangerous thing to say when the punishment for being such a creature was generally to be burnt at the stake or even worse. Thiess, as the man was called, announced that werewolves were, in fact, benevolent creatures of God and he gave them the name 'Hounds of God'. He said that the Hounds of God used their werewolf gifts to protect people. The Hounds of God would do battle with demons and witches in the very depths of hell, preventing them from ascending to earth and wreaking havoc among men and women. Bad crops, he explained, were the result of the werewolves failing to restrain the evil spirits. Thiess was adamant that even though he was a werewolf, he would still go to heaven. Unfortunately, the judges who listened to him did not agree with his views but they decided not to bring the full weight of the law to bear on him, sentencing him to only ten lashes.

THE BENANDANTI

It is said that the old man Thiess was a werewolf of the Benandanti kind. The Benandanti were a particular type of werewolf that did as Thiess claimed - fought evil spirits and demons in the underworld, known as the Malandanti. Their struggles with the Malandanti occurred on four nights of the year, nights that corresponded with the times at which crops were planted or harvested.

The Benandanti were always opposed to witchcraft of any kind, but in 1610 a group of Benandanti werewolves was brought before the Inquisition, the Catholic Church's movement to root out heretics and offenders against the official Church canon. These Benandanti were found guilty of committing acts of witchcraft and of being witches. The Benandanti, thereafter, became the very thing they had always fought against- evil werewolves - although some sources suggest that they had already lost their struggle with the Malandanti and that it was in fact underworld witches that appeared before the Inquisition.

WEREWOLF PANIC

When German priest and theology professor, Martin Luther, pinned his *Ninety-Five Theses* on the door of the Castle Church in Wittenberg on 31 October 1517, launching the Reformation, the very existence of the Catholic Church came under threat. It undertook to protect itself by any means possible. One of these was a campaign of fear in countries loyal to the Pope in Rome, an effort to rid the populace of satanic beliefs and practices.

WEREWOLF TRIALS

Whereas, in the past, St Augustine and St Thomas Aquinas had derided the belief in lycanthropy, around the 13th century, the Church had decided that it was in its best interests to believe that Satan was, indeed, capable of turning people into werewolves or of giving people the power to do so themselves. As a result of this campaign, between 1521 and 1600, a number of men were tried for therianthropy - becoming a wild beast. The first official execution for werewolfism had occurred in Switzerland in 1407 when several accused were tortured and burnt at the stake. But with the Church's focus on reform, an increasing number of cases were brought before the courts. There was little patience with such cases and inquisitors - those appointed by the Church to root out heretics and Satanists - are known to have sometimes dismembered accused people in order to find the incriminating wolf hair inside their bodies. Of course, if there was none to be found, the accused was innocent. Unfortunately, he or she was also dead.

Inward Growing Hair

The sad story is reported, for instance, of a man from the Lombard town of Pavia who attacked a number of men in 1541 and savaged them, apparently in the shape of a wolf. He was eventually caught but assured the people who captured him that the only difference between him and a wolf was that with a real wolf the hair grew outwards, while with him it grew inwards. Naturally, the magistrates were keen to prove the truth of this. So, they cut off his arms and legs to inspect his insides. Needless to say, nothing untoward was found, but the man, of course, died. He suffered from little more than delusions. However, it is worth remembering that the idea of the skin growing in an inwards direction is an ancient one.

Versipellis, or 'skin-turning' can be found in many ancient sources - Petronius, Lucilius and Plautus - and is undoubtedly related to the old Norse word for a shapeshifter or werewolf, *hamrammr*.

The Panic Spreads

Around the same time as the above story, there were said to be so many werewolves in the area around the city of Constantinople (modern-day Istanbul) that the city's ruler led a party of soldiers out into the surrounding countryside and attacked them, killing, it is reported, around 150. The 16th-century French jurist, Jean Bodin told the story of the Royal Procurator-General who claimed to have fired an arrow into the thigh of a wolf and that later a man had been found in bed with an arrow lodged in his thigh. Bodin also quoted from a treatise on sorcerers by Pierre Marner in which the author claims to have seen men transformed into wolves in Savoy. Another report around the time tells of a woodcutting peasant being attacked by a wolf in a village near Lucerne in Switzerland. He defended himself, chopping off one of the creature's legs at which point it transformed into a woman, but a woman missing an arm. She was burnt alive. A great deal of criminal behaviour was at the time attributed to the devil or demons who, it was said, enabled criminal acts to be carried out while the perpetrator was disguised as an animal. Other people were thought merely to have been cursed with the compulsion of being an animal and they also had the desire to consume flesh and drink their victims' blood.

Authorities Warnings

The authorities that governed France's rural areas, actually issued proclamations warning people to be aware of the dangers of werewolves and providing instructions on how to arrest and punish such creatures when they were discovered to be abroad. They looked upon shapeshifters as citizens who were leading depraved existences, endangering others with their habits. The authorities' entreaties were not entirely successful, however. In some rural parts of France, mystical and supernatural practices actually flourished rather than declined. Shapeshifting was looked upon by many as a blessing rather than a curse. Of course, a pact with the devil also excused a great deal of bad behaviour on the part of many, especially those with a strong sex drive.

The opportunity was often seized to falsely accuse people against whom a grudge was being harboured or with whom the accuser was in a dispute of some kind. In this manner, it was a situation not unlike the witchcraft and sorcery trials in England. In such febrile times, it was relatively simple to dream up a testimony and have someone convicted. After all, the witnesses were rarely, if at all, subjected to a particularly searching cross-examination and the court was usually biased against what they saw as an untrustworthy and devious accused. If the accused was a notable or distinguished person, there was some leeway - it was invariably put down to delusion or hysteria. However, if it was just an ordinary citizen who was accused, torture on the rack or by some other means was always likely to produce a confession.

PIERRE BURGOT AND MICHAEL VERDUN

Werewolf transformations never occurred in court or before unbiased witnesses. They were effected in remote locations and in the presence, more often than not of unreliable witnesses. Nonetheless, in France around 30,000 cases of werewolf 'infection' were reported. One of the earliest and most famous werewolf trials took place in 1521. Pierre Burgot and Michel Verdun, were tried before the Domincans at Poligny in the diocese of Alençon.

Burgot told the court that 19 years previously, while he was tending his sheep, there was a violent storm during which they were dispersed across the countryside. He was trying in vain to herd them back together again when three black horsemen rode up. When he explained his predicament, one of the horsemen told him not to worry, that his master would look after them for him. All he had to do was pledge allegiance to this master. They agreed to meet again in a few days

and Burgot walked on, delighted shortly after to discover his flock herded together. When he met the dark stranger a few days later, he told the court, he learned that his master was, in fact, the devil. Burgot agreed to forswear God and Christianity and ally himself with Satan. After two years of not attending church, a time during which he prospered and had no further problems with his sheep, he resumed church attendance. However, around that time, a man named Michel Verdun brought him back into the devil's fold, offering him money.

The Transformation

He attended a witches' Sabbath at which he was smeared with a salve that transformed him into a wolf. He was exceptionally strong in this form and was able to run like the wind. Later, another salve was administered and he returned to his human form. In the years following, he undertook a number of expeditions in the shape of a wolf, expeditions after which, he explained to the court he was so exhausted that he remained in bed for days. He described an attack on a boy of six or seven years old who screamed so loudly that he had to rapidly regain his human form in order to avoid detection. On another occasion a four-year-old girl was the victim. All of her, apart from one arm, was devoured and her flesh was described by Burgot as delicious. Another girl was strangled and her blood drunk, while only a part of the stomach was eaten of another. Their bloodlust became so great that they could not stop killing. To the horror of the friars, they also admitted to having sexual relations with female wolves. Naturally, such evidence was compelling. The two men were found guilty of sorcery and summarily executed.

Around the same time, a hunter was reported to have wounded a wolf with his sword and to have followed its bloody trail through the forest where he had encountered it. The trail led to a small hut but when he crashed in, intent on killing the beast, he discovered a peasant, Michel Udon, with a wound being bathed by a woman, presumably his wife. The peasant was arrested and executed, as were two other men, Philibert Montot and another man known as Gros Pierre, who confessed along with him, undoubtedly after a spell on the rack.

JACQUES ROLLET

In 1598, Jacques Rollet was accused after two hunters had come across two wolves feeding on the carcass of a 15-year-old boy. The wolves had scattered when they were interrupted but, the men who were armed, pursued them. Strangely, however, they later claimed, as they followed them, that the paw-prints slowly changed into those of a human. They eventually caught up with and apprehended their quarry who turned out to be a tall, gaunt man with long, matted hair and a thick beard, dressed in dirty rags that hung in tatters from his body. They noticed that his hands were covered in blood and what appeared to be human flesh was stuck in his long fingernails.

He told them his name was Jacques Rollet and confessed on the spot to being in possession of an ointment that, when he smeared it on his body, transformed him into a wolf. He admitted that, as a wolf, he had attacked many children and eaten them but that he had only done it because he was poor and his family was starving. Interestingly, although he was sentenced to death, the verdict was overruled by the Parlement of Paris on the grounds that his mind was deranged and he was, therefore, unfit to plead. Instead of being executed, he was confined to a hospital for the rest of his life. This decision perhaps marked the beginning of the growing belief that behaving like a wolf could be explained by medical reasons rather than supernatural ones.

Illicit Relations with Demons

In the midst of this hysteria, women were not excluded from suspicion. Francois Secretain was executed after she confessed to taking part in rituals in which other women as well as children and animals had been killed and with having illicit relations with a demon. The process was always the same, however. A woman or a child would be found, apparently savaged by wild beasts. Reports of wolves being seen in the vicinity would be brought to the attention of the authorities. Suspects would be rounded up and confessions would inevitably follow the hideous torture they were forced to endure. Trial and inevitable execution ensued.

The true explanation for many of the deaths of the victims in these cases was, of course, that they had probably been killed and eaten by real wolves. But it appears that communities, gripped by a kind of hysteria, were forced to come up with scapegoats for the deaths and that the executions of these scapegoats would somehow purge them of the evil that they feared was in their midst.

By 1603, around 600 alleged shapeshifters had been burned at the stake and there was no end to the trials and executions as the decades passed, despite opposition to them being increasingly voiced by influential people.

REAL
WEREW

LYCANTHROPY IN MEDICINE

Lycanthropy is a word that combines the Greek words *lukos*, meaning wolf - and *anthropos*, meaning man or mankind. Interestingly, as well as meaning the state of werewolfism, lycanthropy - or 'clinical lycanthropy' as it is often termed to separate it from the werewolf legend - is also a medical term that describes a rare mental illness in which a patient believes that he or she has been transformed into an animal and behaves according to the characteristics of that animal.

Lycanthropy does not specifically refer to the transformation from human to wolf and indeed the characteristics of a wide variety of creatures have been experienced by sufferers. There have been reports of people who believed themselves to have been transformed into wolves or dogs, but cases have also been reported of a hyena, a cat, a horse, a bird, a tiger and even frogs and bees. One person studied in 1989, believed himself to have been changed from human to dog, then to horse and finally to cat form.

A SUPERABUNDANCE OF MELANCHOLIE

Clinical lycanthropy is believed to be brought on by various conditions, amongst which are schizophrenia, bipolar disorder and clinical depression. Interestingly, King James I of England was of the opinion that lycanthropy was a delusion caused by a 'superabundance of melancholie' (it did not stop him believing that witches could turn into cats, foxes or hares, however!).

In 1621, English scholar, Robert Burton, wrote in his *Anatomie of Melancholy*:

> Lycanthropia, which Avicenna calls Cucubuth, others Lupinam Insaniam or Wolf-Madness, when men run howling about graves and fields in the night, and will not be persuaded but that they are wolves or some such beasts. Aetius and Paulus call it a kind of melancholy; but I should rather refer to it as madness, as most do. This malady is nowadays frequent in Bohemia and Hungary. Schernitzius will have it in common in Livonia. They lie hid most part all day, and go abroad in the night, barking, howling, at graves and deserts; they have usually hollow eyes, scabbed legs and thighs and unquenchable thirst and are very dry and pale.

In studies of clinical lycanthropy, it is also believed that an important factor may be

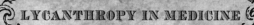

alterations in the parts of the brain that are involved in representing body shape. The reports from professionals who have studied those suffering with clinical lycanthropy show that the patient really is experiencing their own body changing; the body image becomes distorted in the patient's mind and it seems absolutely real to them.

FRIGHTENING SEIZURES

The famous 16th century Dutch physician, Petrus Forestus, is reported to have examined a peasant at Alkmaar who, every spring, could be found running around the local church and its cemetery, wielding a staff with which he fended off the dogs that were constantly attacking him. By the time the physician got to him, he was covered in scars and his eyes were hollow, his face pale. Forestus examined him and declared him to be a lycanthropist, although it was never claimed that the man changed shape in any way during these frightening seizures. It is likely, therefore, that he believed himself to have taken on the shape of a wolf, although outwardly he retained his human form.

MODERN CASES OF LYCANTHROPY

Of course, not everyone suffering from lycanthropy, or werewolfism, will kill. The 1970s *Canadian Psychiatric Association Journal* recorded some extraordinary cases. There was 21-year-old Mr H who believed that if he consumed a mixture of LSD and strychnine, he would be transformed into a wolf. He claimed to have actually had fur grow on his hands and face and had experienced a bloodlust, leading him to want to eat live rabbits. He was hearing voices in his head that he claimed were from Satan and was convinced that he possessed supernatural powers. He was diagnosed as suffering from toxic psychosis and was treated with antipsychotic medicine. He left treatment, but has not been seen since.

Mr W

Mr W, a 37-year-old, was in the habit of howling at the moon, growing his hair and beard long and sleeping outside. Revealed to be suffering from deterioration of the cerebral tissue, he was treated with antipsychotic drugs but his mental capabilities were seriously damaged by his psychosis.

Ms B

A woman, 49-year-old Ms B, constantly fantasized about wolves, ultimately believing that she was becoming one. At a party, she was liable to take off all her clothes and go down on all fours and once she was even found gnawing at bedposts. Believing herself to be possessed by the devil, she underwent a programme of treatment that appeared to help her condition, although she still reverted to her terrifying psychosis every time there was a full moon. For instance, she claimed that when she looked into a mirror, looking back at her was the head of a wolf. Happily, she was eventually cured of her condition.

Bill Ramsey

Those people were lucky. They were treated for their psychosis. Sometimes, it is more complicated. A man named Bill Ramsey had suffered from strange sensations and rage-filled seizures from the age of nine. They were usually accompanied by a foul-

smelling odour and a compulsion to snap and bite like a rabid dog. He successfully restrained his urges until he was an adult but in 1983, while being treated in a hospital in London, he snapped. One day, he made a sudden lunge for a nurse and bit her. He is then reported to have run to a corner of the room in which he was being treated and got down on all fours, barking and growling at anyone who dared to approach him. The police arrived and a number of officers were able to restrain him long enough to inject him with a sedative. He was taken from the hospital to a psychiatric institution where his condition continued to puzzle doctors.

Paranormal Investigators

Two well-known paranormal investigators and demonologists, Ed and Lorraine Warren, who had been involved in several notorious cases of haunting such as the infamous Amityville Horror, began to take an interest in the case. Their theory was that Ramsey was in fact possessed by a 'werewolf demon' and that it would have to be exorcised. Ramsey was taken to Connecticut and Bishop Robert McKenna was engaged to carry out the exorcism. Just in case things got out of hand, they also invited four police officers. Ramsey was immensely strong when 'possessed' and they were afraid of the damage he might do if he were to break free.

The ceremony began, a crucifix being applied to Ramsey's body and the appropriate prayers and incantations being recited. The bishop commanded the demon to leave Ramsey's body and Ramsey, who before the ceremony had begun had expressed his belief that it was nonsense, had to be prevented by the police officers from attacking him. Despite his scepticism, however, it seems to have had an effect and Ramsey has

stated since that he did indeed experience something akin to a force leaving his body. Whatever took place that night, after the ritual he was free of the terrifying psychosis from which he had been suffering.

DARK DELUSIONS

In *Vampires, Werewolves and Demons*, Dr Richard Knoll records 18 documented cases since 1975 of people who have suffered from the delusion that they were animals - known as zoanthropy or therianthropy. Six of these cases involved wolves.

In an issue of the British academic journal *Psychological Medicine* from 1988, the study of 12 patients suffering from lycanthropy is discussed. Lycanthropic conditions are described that had a duration of between a single day and 13 years. Most of the patients involved had eventually been diagnosed with delusional depression or schizophrenia, although the subjects were often also suffering from other disorders. Most recovered from their condition and only two of the patients were totally unresponsive to treatment. The study concluded that, 'Like other curious and memorable syndromes...lycanthropy persists as an occasional but colorful feature of severe and occasionally factitious psychosis. However, it appears that the delusion of being transformed into an animal may bode no more ill than any other delusion.' Of course, stories passed down through the ages often dispute that claim.

MODERN RESEARCH

Modern researchers have explained away the werewolf phenomenon by ascribing other recognized medical conditions to it. In 1963, Dr Lee Illis of Guy's Hospital in London delivered a paper entitled *On Porphyria and the Aetiology of Werwolves*. Dr Illis suggests in his paper that werewolves described in historical accounts could in fact have been suffering from congenital porphyria. The condition's symptoms - photosensitivity, reddish teeth, excessive hair growth and psychosis, would have been sufficient reason for accusing someone of being a werewolf.

FREAK SHOWS

Others have suggested that people accused of being werewolves might actually have been afflicted by hypertrichosis which is a bizarre condition in which the sufferer experiences excessive hair growth. Alternatively known as *Wolfitis*, hypertrichosis results in large amounts of hair growing in unusual places all over the body, including the entire face. In the 19th century, sufferers often made a living by becoming part of 'freak shows' in carnivals or circuses. They would appear under names such as 'dog-man', 'wolf-girl', 'wolf-man' or simply 'werewolf'.

Woodcut of a father and son with excessive, unnatural facial hair. Aldrovandi, 1642.

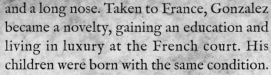

AMBRAS SYNDROME

We are all covered in long, fair hair (lanugo) before birth but this generally falls out towards the end of the pregnancy. In very few cases, it remains until a baby is about a year old and then falls out. However, in some very rare cases it continues to grow throughout the sufferer's life. Petrus Gonzalez, born in the Canary Isles in 1556, was the first recorded case of what is known as Ambras Syndrome, where the hair keeps growing on unexpected parts of the body throughout life. Hair grows on the nose, ears and even on the eyelids and there are further associated complications such as extra teeth

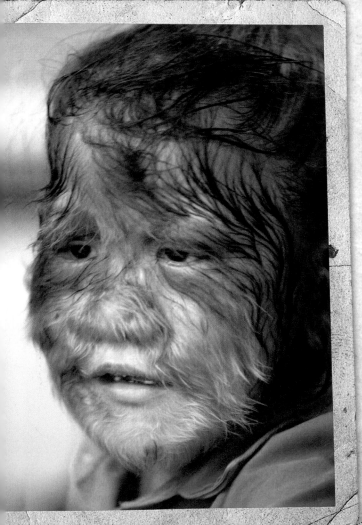

and a long nose. Taken to France, Gonzalez became a novelty, gaining an education and living in luxury at the French court. His children were born with the same condition.

Another form of the condition, hypertrichosis terminalis is the condition where hair grows over the entire body and it is fully coloured unlike the fair lanugo. There is no known cure for this condition which is inevitably known as Werewolf Syndrome. Today, there are about 20 sufferers of Werewolf Syndrome, mostly from the Aceves family from Loreto in Mexico. They travel with the Mexican National Circus and are known as the Wolf People. Jesus 'Chuy' Acaves has the condition, as does his daughter Karla.

Some forms of this dreadful illness appear after the sufferer has experienced a trauma or a shock of some kind. Starvation or the common modern condition anorexia nervosa, or excessive drug use can induce it, although it is more often an inherited condition that people are simply born with. One commentator has noted, however, that hypertrichosis was unlikely to be behind those suspected of being werewolves because the condition is extremely rare and sightings of werewolves in medieval Europe were far from rare.

The disease of rabies is also put forward as the source for werewolf beliefs. The symptoms of that disease are remarkably similar to the behaviour of a werewolf and rabies is, after all, caught by being bitten by a rabid creature. Interestingly, however, the idea of werewolfism being transmitted as a result of a bite is a relatively recent one and does not form part of the original myths and legends. In the old days, if a werewolf bit you, you were likely to end up dead and eaten.

Thai schoolgirl Supatra Sasuphan who suffers from the very rare Ambras syndrome.

FREUD'S WOLF MAN

The Wolf Man, whose real name was Sergei Pankejeff, was one of the most famous patients of Dr Sigmund Freud, the founder of psychoanalysis. Pankejeff was a deeply troubled Russian aristocrat who began treatment under Dr Freud in 1910.

After an extended period of analysis, Freud published his history of the case, calling his patient 'The Wolf Man' to protect his identity, and also because he believed Pankejeff's recurring dream, in which he saw a pack of wolves sitting in a tree, was deeply significant. The case became a groundbreaking one in the history of psychoanalysis; in it, Freud claimed the importance of childhood experiences in the development of the adult psyche, and laid particular emphasis on infantile sexual awakening - a shocking notion at the time he was writing.

Sergei Pankejeff came from a wealthy St Petersburg family, and was well educated, having spent time studying in Russia and Germany. However, the family had a history of mental instability, which was exacerbated by the political turmoil in Russia at the time. Sergei's older sister Anna, who was schizophrenic, killed herself in 1906. The following year, his father Konstantin also took his life. Sergei, who was in Munich at the time of his father's death, became deeply depressed, and sought help from a number of psychiatrists to alleviate his condition.

Two Suicides

In 1910, Pankejeff's personal physician brought him to Vienna for treatment with Dr Sigmund Freud, who was gaining a name for himself as a neurologist specializing in psychosomatic illnesses. As well as his depression, Pankejeff was suffering from various debilitating physical symptoms, such as chronic constipation (he was only able to pass a motion with the help of an enema), and disturbed vision (he felt as though he was looking at the world through a misty veil). He was unable to look after himself, and needed several attendants.

Despite Pankejeff's distress and his urgent need for help, Freud found his new patient very passive: his attitude was one of indifference, and he was highly resistant to analysis. Contrary to Freud's usual practice, he gave Pankejeff a deadline of a year to complete the therapy, hoping that this would spur him on. Having this deadline, Freud believed, helped Pankejeff to co-operate with the treatment.

Six White Wolves

In 1899, Freud had published his book *The Interpretation of Dreams*, setting out his theory that the apparently chaotic material we remember from dreams is in fact highly significant, and can be interpreted to give us an account of the secret motives and desires of our unconscious mind. These desires, Freud claimed, are mainly sexual, and difficult to access, because society requires us to repress them in our waking lives. Accordingly, Freud centred his treatment of Pankejeff around a recurring dream that had troubled him from childhood. Paying attention to the exact wording, narrative, and imagery his patient used, Freud recounted Pankejeff's dream thus:

> I dreamt that it was night and that I was lying in bed ... Suddenly the window opened of its own accord and I was terrified to see that some white wolves were sitting on the big walnut tree in front of the window. There were six or seven of them. The wolves were quite white, and looked more like foxes or sheepdogs ... In great terror, evidently of being eaten up by the wolves, I screamed and woke up. My nurse hurried to my bed, to see what had happened to me. It took quite a long while before I was convinced that it had only been a dream; I had such a clear and life-like picture of the window opening and the wolves sitting on the tree.

As well as recounting the dream, Pankejeff drew a picture of the wolves sitting in the tree. Strangely, there were only five wolves in his picture, rather than the six or seven that he had described in his account of the dream.

The Primal Scene

Freud's analysis of the dream, which was very unorthodox, was that the wolves represented the patient's father, and that the dream sprang from an unconscious memory that the young child had had, in which he had seen his parents copulating. Freud thought it likely that the child had come into his parents' room and saw them having sex, with his father taking his mother from behind. A misunderstanding of the situation, involving a fear of castration, and a primitive sexual desire towards his father, had caused the child's sexuality to become confused, and a deep neurosis to spring into being, which had persisted into adulthood. For this reason, Freud called his notes on The Wolf Man case, *From the History of an Infantile Neurosis*.

According to Freud's account, his extended treatment of The Wolf Man proved beneficial, and as a result, Pankejeff was relieved of many of his more troubling symptoms. He went on to become one of Freud's most celebrated patients, and something of an example of the positive effects of psychoanalysis. Often cited by Freud as proof of the efficacy of the 'talking cure', Pankejeff later revealed his identity as The Wolf Man, and collaborated with Freudian psychoanalysts until his death in 1979.

Success or Failure?

There were some critics of Freud who pointed out that the treatment of The Wolf Man was by no means as successful as had been claimed. Witnesses told how, a few years after the treatment, Pankejeff had been seen walking the streets of Vienna looking in a mirror, under the delusion that a doctor had drilled a hole in his nose. Needless to say, this caused some doubt about how effective the 'talking cure' had been in his case. Others, such as Austrian journalist Karin Obholzer, who interviewed Pankejeff in the

1970s, claimed that The Wolf Man himself did not believe the conclusion Freud had come to in his analysis of the dream. Pankejeff said that he had no memory of seeing his parents copulating, and that it was most unlikely that he would ever have witnessed such an event. In wealthy Russian families, young children would not have barged in on their parents in that way. They would have slept in their nannies' bedrooms, he said, and would never have witnessed their parents engaged in sexual activity, or gone to them for help when waking in the night.

Family Trauma

Initially, Pankejeff remarked, he had believed Freud's analysis, and had waited for the childhood memory to come to him, but it never did. Over the years, he had drawn the conclusion that Freud had misdiagnosed him, and that the basis of his neurosis was nothing to do with witnessing a primal scene between his parents at a young age, but concerned his tortured relationship to his dead sister. And indeed, it does seem likely, on the face of it, that the two suicides in Pankejeff's immediate family - his sister's, and his father's - would be far more disturbing to him than a putative sexual memory from his early childhood.

The Wolf Man case was later reinterpreted by psychoanalysts Maria Torok and Nicolas Abraham in their book *The Wolf Man's Magic Word*, in which they show how the multilingual nature of Pankejeff's background could have influenced the content of his dream. They point out that the Russian word for sister, 'siestorka', is similar to the Russian phrase 'pack of six', 'shiestorka', and, using a novel concept that they called 'cryptonymy', concluded that, far from being about Pankejeff's relationship with his

parents, the wolves may have symbolized his sister, and his desire to have her back alive and watching over him.

Freud's Legacy

Later, The Wolf Man case was discussed by philosophers Gilles Deleuze and Felix Guattari, who argued that Freud's insistence on the sexual cause of all neurosis was over-simplistic, and that he had been too reductive in his thinking. They also brought up evidence to show that Pankejeff had been in and out of treatment for decades after his sessions with Freud, and that he had declared his analysis to have been a catastrophe. Today, it seems likely that Freud overstated the success of The Wolf Man case, and that his focus on significance of the primal scene that the young Pankejeff supposedly witnessed was wrong. However, it cannot be denied that parts of the analysis were groundbreaking, and that by looking at the source of neurosis in childhood experience, Freud showed great insight. His emphasis on listening carefully to what his patients told him, and in paying attention to psychic material such as dreams, which had previously been ignored in the treatment of mental illness, was also revolutionary - and essentially humane in its approach.

Thus, Freud's celebrated analysis of The Wolf Man, despite its many apparent errors, remains one of the founding texts of psychoanalysis, and continues to this day to excite controversy and debate, containing as it does some of Freud's most important theories about the universal nature of infantile sexuality, castration anxiety, the Oedipus complex, repression, and the division of the mind into the id, ego, and superego.

Timber wolves (Canis lupus) fighting over a carcass.

THE FULL MOON KILLER

It was 1985 and 32 people had died in Florence in the past 17 years, the majority of them killed during the full moon. They were mainly courting couples, murdered and mutilated in cars parked on lonely streets. They were shot through the vehicle's windows and a sharp implement, suspected to be a scalpel, was used to mutilate them after death, sex organs or breasts often being removed.

Double Murder

It had begun in August 1968 when a man and his mistress were shot dead close to a cemetery in the suburbs of Florence. The woman was married and a jealous husband was immediately suspected. He was arrested and confessed. Convicted of the double murder, he was sent to prison. Shortly after, however, he withdrew his confession, but no one believed him. He had been arrested, after all, leaving his house the day after the murders carrying a suitcase. It seemed the case was closed, but six years later, on 14 September 1974, there was another shooting in Florence. Again a couple courting in their car on a deserted street, were murdered and mutilated, the woman having been stabbed 96 times. To everyone's surprise, the .22 bullets, fired from a Berreta pistol, matched those that had killed the couple in 1968.

The Monster of Florence

Seven years passed before the next incident on 6 June 1981. A couple was again killed in their car and the woman's genitals were mutilated. They began to call the killer the 'Monster of Florence'. A homosexual couple died in 1983, killed by bullets from the same Berreta as the previous murders. There was no mutilation in this case and investigators pondered whether the killer had made a mistake, believing the people in the car to be a courting man and woman. Following the last murders in 1985, the assistant prosecutor received an envelope containing strips of flesh, carved from the breast of the last woman to be killed.

A Suspect is Identified

The investigation had been exhaustive over the 17 years since the first murders and more than 100,000 people had been questioned in connection with the case. It was only in the early 1990s that suspicion began to fall on a 68-year-old farmer, Pietro Pacciani, whose hobby was taxidermy. He had already served a prison term for stabbing and stamping a man to death and had been known to

have sexually molested his own daughters. Interestingly, however, he was involved in an occult group. Pacciani maintained his innocence throughout and the evidence against him was slight, but he was convicted of seven murders. While he was freed on appeal, however, two of his associates, Mario Vanni and Giancarlo Lotti, were arrested and convicted for their part in five of the murders.

Although the public and the media were convinced of his guilt, Pacciani was granted a re-trial but before the case could return to court, he died of a drug overdose. The fact that these murders were committed under a full moon and in something of a frenzy, coupled with Pacciani's interest in the occult has convinced many that werewolf-like tendencies were at play, but the truth of that died with him.

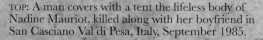
TOP: A man covers with a tent the lifeless body of Nadine Mauriot, killed along with her boyfriend in San Casciano Val di Pesa, Italy, September 1985.

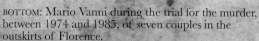
BOTTOM: Mario Vanni during the trial for the murder, between 1974 and 1985, of seven couples in the outskirts of Florence.

ALBERT FISH
THE WEREWOLF OF WYSTERIA

A paedophile, a sadist and a cannibal killer with evil bestial urges, Albert Fish has been pronounced by experts to be the most deranged human being ever. When questioned by police, Fish explained that he became 'uncontrollably transformed by a sort of blood thirst within me'. Once it was done, he was distraught.

'I would have given my life within half-an-hour of having done it to restore her life,' he said.

Violent character metamorphosis followed by unremitting remorse are typical signs of the classic werewolf psychosis. Albert Fish showed all the undeniable symptoms of being the ultimate lycan.

The Burning Wolf Within

Known as the Werewolf of Wysteria, the Grey Man, the Brooklyn Vampire and The Boogeyman, Albert Fish was an American serial killer and cannibal. He claimed to have eaten and molested children all over the United States. Although Fish was suspected of at least 15 murders, he eventually confessed to three. He claimed to have committed another 100 crimes against children. Whenever the dark werewolf rage within him was released, this seemingly harmless, grey-haired old man was transformed into a terrifying flesh-ripping beast.

Cannibal killer, Albert Fish, on his arrest in 1905.

He loved inflicting pain and to have pain inflicted on himself. He inserted needles into his body, in the area of the groin and perineum; after his eventual arrest, twenty-nine were discovered by an X-ray. He inserted alcohol-coated balls of cotton wool into his anus; he would then ignite them to 'cleanse himself of his sins'. He perpetrated the same gruesome acts and even worse on his child victims. At his trial, the jury took less than an hour to reach a guilty verdict. Fish thanked the judge for his sentence of death by electrocution. A *Daily News* reporter wrote, 'his watery eyes gleamed at the thought of being burned by a heat more intense than the flames with which he often seared his flesh to gratify his lust.'

On 16 January 1936, Albert Fish was executed at Sing Sing maximum security prison in New York state, he was strapped into 'Old Sparky', the electric chair, and three minutes later, was dead. He is reported to have said that electrocution would be 'the supreme thrill of my life'.

Childhood Whippings

Albert Fish was born Hamilton Fish in 1870 and his father was 43 years older than his mother. When his father died in 1875, the five-year-old Hamilton was put into St John's Orphanage by his mother. It was there that he changed his name to Albert to avoid the nickname 'Ham and Fish' that he had been given by the other children.

Life in the orphanage was harsh and cruel. There were regular beatings and whippings, but, perversely, Albert grew to enjoy the pain. He enjoyed it so much, in fact, that he would have erections for which the other children mocked him. His mother was able to look after him again when she found employment in 1879, but Albert was already

scarred by his experiences at St John's. By the age of 12, he was engaged in a homosexual relationship. His partner, a telegraph boy, introduced him to perverse practices such as coprophagia and drinking urine. He spent his weekends watching boys undress at the public baths.

Male Prostitute

Fish claimed that by 1890 he was working as a male prostitute in New York City and that he was raping young boys on a regular basis. In 1898 he married and fathered six children. He was working as a house painter but was also molesting countless children, mostly boys under the age of six. At this time, he developed an interest in castration and wanted to experiment on a man with whom he had been having a relationship; the man fled before Fish could carry it out.

His life changed completely, in 1917, when his wife ran off with another man. Fish began to behave even more strangely than before. He claimed to hear voices and once wrapped himself up in a carpet, saying he had been ordered to do so by St John. His children reported seeing him beat himself on his nude body with a nail-studded piece of wood until he was covered with blood. Once they saw him standing alone on a hill with his hands raised, shouting: 'I am Christ.'

The Wolf in the Woods

In 1924, seven-year-old Francis McDonnell was playing with some friends near his home on Staten Island. His mother saw a man behaving oddly. He walked up and down the street, wringing his hands and talking to himself. She thought no more of him and went indoors. Later that same day, the same man lured Francis into some nearby woods. The next day his body was discovered, sexually brutalized, mauled, mutilated and strangled. It would be another 10 years before police would uncover that the killer was Albert Fish.

In 1927, Fish abducted Billy Gaffney. He tortured and killed him in a bestial frenzy. Fish later retold the story with relish:

I whipped his bare ass till the blood ran from his legs. I cut off his ears, nose, slit his mouth from ear to ear. Gouged out his eyes. He was dead then. I stuck the knife in his belly and held my mouth to his body and drank his blood.

But it was the killing of Grace Budd that led to Fish's eventual capture. When Fish was 58 years old, he arrived on the Budds' doorstep in May 1928, pretending to be

Investigators gathering evidence near the deserted Westchester house where Albert Fish murdered Grace Budd.

Frank Howard, a farmer from Farmingdale, New York. He was calling in response to an advert placed in the *New York World* by Edward Budd, Grace's 18-year-old brother, asking for work.

The Wolf Returns

Fish spun a story that he needed someone to work on his farm and Edward was eager to oblige. Fish returned a few days later to confirm that Edward had the job and was asked to stay for lunch. While there, Fish befriended Grace. She sat on his lap at the dinner table. Just like the wolf in the story of *Little Red Riding Hood*, Albert Fish decided to eat the little girl. As he was about to leave, he said he was on his way to a children's birthday party at his sister's house and wondered whether Grace would like to accompany him. Grace's mother was unsure, but her husband thought it would be fun for the girl and off Grace went with Albert Fish. It was the last they saw of their daughter.

He took the unsuspecting Grace on a train to the Bronx and then to the village of Worthington in Westchester. For Grace, he only bought a one-way ticket. Grace was enthralled with the 40-minute ride into the countryside. Only twice in her life had she been out of the city. This was a wonderful treat for her. They walked along a remote road until they reached an abandoned two-storey building called Wysteria Cottage in the midst of a wooded area. Fish went up to the second floor bedroom and took off his clothes. He reset the scene:

When she saw me all naked she began to cry and tried to run down the stairs. I grabbed her and she said she would tell her mamma. First I stripped her naked. How she did kick — bite and scratch. I choked her to death, then cut her in small pieces so I could take my meat to my rooms. Cook and eat it. How sweet and tender her little ass was roasted in the oven. It took me 9 days to eat her entire body.

An Uncontrollable Bestial Rage

Ultimately, it was Fish's arrogance that betrayed him. He wrote a letter to Grace's mother six years later boasting about the killing. The letter was delivered in an envelope that bore the logo of the New York Private Chauffeur's Benevolent Association. It turned out that a janitor of the association had left some stationery in a boarding house when he had moved out. Albert Fish had moved in after him. Detective William F. King waited at the house and when Fish arrived he asked him to accompany him to police HQ to answer some questions. Fish lunged at King with a razor, but the policeman easily overpowered him and arrested him.

Fish confessed to the murder of Grace Budd launching a debate as to whether the violently uncontrollable, bestial rages within him proved he was innocent, but with an insane split personality. However, he was found to be both sane and guilty and was sentenced to death. After sentencing he confessed to the murder of Francis McDonnell. Between the years of 1924 and 1932, as well as the three beast-like murders that can be ascribed to him, the Werewolf of Wysteria may have hunted down and assaulted hundreds more children. Finally, in 1936, the electric chair at Sing Sing made sure that the wolf within Albert Fish would hunt no more.

ANDREI CHIKATILO
THE RIPPER OF ROSTOV

Rostov-on-Don is a famous seaport on the river Don in Russia, but it was also the scene for the worst serial killings in Russian history. The Ripper of Rostov killed at least 53 young women and children, cannibalizing the bodies of many of his victims.

From the late 1970s to the early 1990s, Andrei Chikatilo, a seemingly mild-mannered teacher, carried out most of his brutal killings in the forests of Russia. Using his daytime professorial persona to entrap his victims and fool the police, he became transformed into a psychopathic beast once he smelled the blood of the kill.

Scarred for Life

Andrei Romanovich Chikatilo was born on 16 October 1936 in Yablochnoye, a village in the heart of rural Ukraine. The Soviet Union, and the Ukraine in particular, suffered a period of great upheaval during the 1930s. His family suffered greatly during Stalin's enforced collectivization and were subjected to extreme poverty and hunger. Before Andrei was born, his older brother, Stefan, went missing in 1931. His mother alleged that Stefan was murdered and eaten by neighbours. Whether this story was true or not, Andrei's mother constantly warned him not to stray from the backyard or he might also be eaten by cannibals. A horrific seed had been planted in his young imagination and later in life, the death of his brother would propel Chikatilo to reap all kinds of cannibalistic vengeance on the population of Rostov-on-Don.

A Lonely Childhood

As a solitary child he inhabited his own fantasy world and was constantly bullied at school by the other kids for being gangly, awkward, effeminate and shy. Desperately short-sighted, he refused to wear spectacles for fear of further ridicule and he kept his bedwetting habit a closely guarded secret.

A deep inner rage began to develop within Chikatilo at the taunts of his classmates. In revenge he captured and killed some of the children's pets. He tortured the cats and dogs while they were still alive by stabbing out their eyes, and cutting off their ears and noses, before chopping them into little pieces. He loved to fantasize about torture scenes in which he replaced the pets with their human owners. No one suspected, however, that this very troubled, introverted little child with a serious sadist streak would develop into one of the worst cannibal serial killers the world has ever known.

Russian serial killer Andrei Chikatilo (1936 - 1994), Rostov, Russia, 1990. Chikatilo was convicted and executed for the murders of more than 50 people over a twelve year period.

Sadistic Kicks and Teenage Fantasies

Chikatilo's first sexual experience as a teenager was when he fumbled with a 10-year-old friend of his sister, pinning her to ground by lying on top of her and slapping her face to make her submit. During the violent wrestling and struggle, he ejaculated over her dress. That struggle and ultimate sexual satisfaction pointed the way ahead for him and remained implanted in his brain as much as any of his torture fantasies. Andrei was now starting to recognize that it was the experience of perpetrating violence on others that he craved much more than the sexual act itself.

After leaving school, he failed the entrance exam for Moscow University and decided to join the army. He got a job as a telephone engineer in the town of Rodionovo-Nesvatayevsky, near Rostov and in 1963, his sister moved in with him. She knew he wasn't all that interested in girls but got him to date one of her friends called Fayina. The unfortunate girl soon realized that her boyfriend was painfully shy and liked weird violent sex. But amazingly they married and did manage to have two children, Lyudmila and Yuri. In 1971,

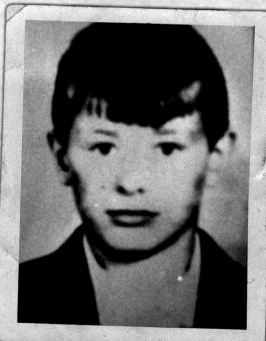

Chikatilo took a correspondence course and obtained degrees in Engineering, Russian and Marxism-Leninism. With these new qualifications, he was able to get a job as a school teacher. As a teacher he was lacking in confidence and was unable to keep his pupils under control. But he came alive and excited when the young girls and boys were within touching distance, and before long he began to commit indecent sexual acts.

At first, he fondled the girls during swimming lessons, putting his hands between their legs until they screamed. Then he kept a 14-year-old girl behind after class for detention and beat her with a ruler until he ejaculated on the floor. His inner animal frustrations and fantasies were escalating until finally, on 22 December 1978, his demons broke out of control and the Ripper of Rostov claimed his first victim.

The First Smell of Young Blood

One day, he lured nine-year-old Lena Zakotnova to a vacant house beside the river where she was forced to the ground and her clothes ripped off. Failing to get an erection or penetrate her, Chikatilo stabbed and slashed her with a knife until he climaxed in a frenzy of sexual ecstasy. Finally ending her life by squeezing the girl's throat until every last breath was out of her. He dumped the mutilated mess of the girl's corpse in the river. The body was discovered two days later. A witness, Svetana Gurenkova, told the police that she had seen Lena with a tall, thin, middle-aged man who had been wearing glasses and a dark coat. They made an artist's impression of the man, and when it was shown to the headmaster of the school, he identified one of his teachers, Andrei Chikatilo. When the police arrived at his house they noticed some specks of blood on the front steps and Chikatilo was taken in for questioning, but later released when his wife gave him an alibi.

Instead, the police arrested a man named Aleksandr Kravchenko, who had a previous conviction for rape. Kravchenko was far too young to fit the description of the man seen with Lena, nor had he ever worn glasses. But he was questioned mercilessly and the police eventually forced a confession out of the innocent man. He was charged for the murder and sentenced to death in 1984. It wasn't until years later when Chikatilo confessed, that the authorities realized that they had executed the wrong man.

The Cannibal Beast is Unleashed

Scared off by this narrow escape, Chikatilo lay low for three years, but in the intervening period his increasingly bizarre sexual behaviour drew attention to himself at the school. Young female pupils complained about his wandering hands and penis flashing. He was eventually fired for trying to push his fingers into a young girl's vagina during a swimming lesson.

Seventeen-year-old Larisa Tkachenko had a reputation as a flirt who willingly had sex with strangers in return for food and drink. In 1981, Chikatilo asked her to go for a drink at a nearby cafe in the woods. Under cover of the treeline, he stripped naked, leapt on her and tried to have sex. The girl laughed at his pathetic attempts to penetrate her with his limp penis. Chikatilo went totally berserk, stabbing, mauling, ripping and biting at her throat, arms, breasts and sexual organs. The beast was finally unleashed. He bit off and swallowed her nipples. She died an excruciatingly painful death under the sustained frenzy of his cannibal-killer attack.

Portraits of four young male murder victims of Andrei Chikatilo. Chikatilo murdered and cannibalized 53 people from 1978 to 1990.

It was the first time that Chikatilo had eaten human flesh. But it was not the last. Slashing his prey wildly with a knife became his horrific trademark. The Ripper's erection grew only when his victims struggled and bled. Then, while they were still breathing, he ejaculated as he ate their sexual organs. Having discovered the hellish secret of the beast within him, his hunger for blood knew no bounds. A month later, 12-year-old Lyuba Biryuk became Chikatilo's third kill. She was stabbed over 40 times and died with knife wounds and bite marks to her eyes, chest, stomach and genitals. The Ripper had sex with the corpse.

Inner Animal Demons Run Riot

Chikatilo's inner demons became uncontrollable, and he regularly hunted down young girls. Victim number four, Laura Sarkisyan, was lured to the woods, savagely slashed and mutilated, and her nipples and genitals eaten. Five more victims followed in the summer of 1983, all found with parts of their bodies bitten off, organs eaten and eyes stabbed out.

By 1984 Chikatilo's lust for blood had reached fever pitch and he killed at least 15 times between January and September of that year, females with their wombs removed outnumbering the boys with their testicles cut off. Always with the eyes stabbed. On 20 October, another woman was found, disembowelled, but, strangely, the organs were nowhere to be found. He had taken them to eat later. Unusually the eyes had not been attacked. Was it the same killer?

A few weeks later another slashed female corpse was found, she had been killed months before and bore all the cannibal hallmarks of the Ripper. Victim number 10 was a 14-year-old boy, found near railway lines. He had been stabbed no fewer than 70 times and had been castrated and raped. The killer had a bowel movement on the body. Semen found in the murdered boy's anus could help the police investigators determine the killer's blood type. They now had a vital clue to the cannibal's identity, and were able to eliminate some suspects. But the killer kept on killing.

Throughout 1984, woods in the region disgorged bodies; lots of them. All with Ripper wounds. A dead 18-year-old girl was found covered with semen and blood after the killer had ejaculated following sex with her corpse. A forensics expert from Moscow confirmed that two semen specimens found on different bodies were type AB and that immediately eliminated every suspect to date. The Ripper was still out there.

The Hunt for the Ripper

In March 1985, he struck again, killing 10-year-old Dmitri Ptashnikov, biting off the tip of his tongue and his penis. Close to the body was a large footprint, the same size thirteen that had been found at an earlier scene. For the first time, however, he was seen. A tall, hollow-cheeked man with a stiff-kneed gait, wearing glasses.

Victims followed in quick succession, one killed by a hammer blow, another stabbed 39 times with a kitchen knife; a mother and daughter killed at the same time; the eyes were stabbed, the heads cut off and sometimes the upper lip and nose were cut off and deposited in the corpse's mouth or stomach. The death toll rose to 24.

The police were lost and confused. Two hundred officers were by this time on the case. They worked undercover at bus and train stations, they walked the streets and parks on the lookout for the tall, hollow-cheeked man. Hidden cameras were set up to

photograph likely suspects; officers working at night were equipped with night-vision goggles. At Rostov bus station, an older man was spotted taking an interest in a young girl. The undercover officer became suspicious and brought him in for questioning. It was Andrei Chikatilo. When questioned about his behaviour, he told police that he was a businessman but had once been a teacher and missed the company of the young. They let him go.

The officer was not totally convinced however, and followed Chikatilo, watching him as he accosted women and even received oral sex from a prostitute in the street; he was picked up again. In his briefcase was a jar of Vaseline, a long knife, a length of rope and a grimy towel. Hardly the office equipment of a businessman. But his blood type was A and not AB. They held him for a few days, but he persisted in his denials. There was nothing untoward in his background and the Ripper was released.

Profile of a Psychokiller

A criminal psychiatrist was asked to create a profile of the killer. He was a sexual deviant, the psychiatrist said, 25 to 50 years old and around five feet ten in height. He was sexually inadequate to the extent that he had to mutilate his victims to achieve arousal. He was a sadist. He damaged the victims' eyes to stop them looking at him or because he believed the old superstition that the image of a killer is left on his victims' eyes. He was a loner and he had sex with corpses.

Stabbing his victims was a way to enter them sexually. He ejaculated, either spontaneously or masturbated with his hand. He cut women's sexual organs as a means of establishing control over them. Organs were often missing, taken as trophies.

The Horror Continues

Then, in August 1985, a dead woman, bearing the usual Ripper marks, was found near Moscow airport. Officers checked flights and tickets, but found nothing. Checking other murders in the capital, however, they found three murders of young boys that seemed in all likelihood to have been committed by the man they were looking for - all had been raped and one had been decapitated. Soon the police were back at Rostov, looking at another slashed young woman, her mouth stuffed with leaves and dirt, her ripped naked body covered in semen and blood. In July and August 1986, two more women's bodies turned up, the second totally buried except for a hand pointing up out of the earth.

In April 1988, a woman was discovered, the tip of her nose sliced off and her skull smashed. Her eyes had not been touched, however. Then a 19-year-old boy was found in May with his penis bitten off. He had been seen entering the woods with a middle-aged man with gold teeth and a sports bag. Even with that lead, the police turned up nothing. In April 1989, a boy's ripped and raped body was found, and in July yet another boy was discovered in the woods with his anus bitten out. Elena Varga was killed in August and that same week, 10-year-old Aleksei Khobotov went missing, his body showing up four months later. A 10-year-old boy was found with his tongue bitten off and in July 1990, a headless 13-year-old was discovered mutilated in the Botanical Gardens.

The fall of Communism in Russia meant newspapers were now free to report on the case and there was a media frenzy with officials desperate for the case to be solved and the killing to stop. When an 11-year-old boy was found stabbed 42 times and castrated, the public were outraged. Another couple of

16-year-old boys were murdered before the police's work at the railway and bus stations, checking the names of passengers, began to bear fruit. Over half-a-million people had been investigated up to this point, but only one name stood out.

The Net Closes Round the Ripper

Andrei Chikatilo had been at Rostov railway station the same day as one of the recent murders. He had been seen emerging from the woods, rubbing his hands to try to clean them. On his cheek was a red smear of blood, his fingers were bleeding and his coat was covered in leaves and twigs. Chikatilo was arrested and a search of his house revealed 23 knives, but nothing linking him with his victims. At first, Chikatilo denied everything, but then he began to admit to 'sexual weakness' and 'perverse sexual activity'.

Finally, he confessed in detail, telling how he could not get an erection and used the knife as a penis substitute getting sexual gratification when he committed violence. 'I had to see blood and wound the victims.' He talked about smearing his semen inside a uterus that he had just removed and as he walked back through the woods, he would chew on it; 'the truffle of sexual murder', as he described it. He would tear at his victims' mouths with his teeth. He said it gave him an 'animal satisfaction' to chew or swallow nipples or testicles.

In all, he confessed to 53 murders stating that as well mutilating the bodies he had eaten the sexual organs and had sex with some of the corpses. When his trial started in Rostov in April 1992, Chikatilo was brought to court and restrained inside a cage of steel bars, like Hannibal Lecter in the movie *Silence of the Lambs*. He screamed and ranted at the courtroom trying to convince the jury he was insane. The judge was unmoved however, and handed down 52 death sentences, dropping one due to 'insufficient evidence'. He ordered that Chikatilo be confined in Rostov's Central Prison until the appointed date of his execution some 18 months later. Legend has it, that by that time, Chikatilo was completely insane.

The End of the Ripper

The Central Prison is in the heart of Rostov and houses a notorious execution chamber - Pistol Target Room No. 3. On 15 February 1994, Chikatilo was taken to the sound-proofed room, strapped into the big wooden execution chair, reportedly struggling and yelling obscenities at the prison guards. The executioner walked silently toward the condemned man from behind the chair. The Ripper was still cursing the world as the gun went off, killing him instantly with a single 9mm bullet behind his right ear. A quicker, much more humane death for Russia's worst serial killer, than any of the torture-filled, protracted last minutes he had inflicted on his ripped-up, half-eaten victims during his reign of cannibal terror in the woods surrounding Rostov.

Andrei Chikatilo, standing trial in April, 1992. During the trial Chikatilo was kept in an iron cage, ironically to protect him from attack by his victims' relatives.

WEREV
of
IMAGI

WOLVES the NATION

WEREWOLVES IN FICTION

Werewolf fiction is a fascinating and diverse body of work that is often deeply rooted in the rich, centuries-old myth and folklore of the werewolf. Depicted in a wide range of vehicles that includes literature's horror magazines, drama, film, television, games and music, the stories told are, of course, more often than not, supernatural tales, designed to entertain and frighten, but there are also symbolic and allegorical tales that are meant to educate or simply warn people against certain practices.

Through the centuries, the depiction of the werewolf has changed greatly. In ancient times, the curse of being a werewolf was often viewed as a punishment for an act of disobedience, both in the eyes of ancient cultures and in the eyes of the early Christians. Stories of St Patrick turning Welsh King Vereticus into a werewolf for rejecting Christianity bear witness to that. Then, by medieval times, as the Catholic Church fought against the growing success of the Reformation, werewolves became loathed creatures, in league with the devil, and a symbol of what happened to you if you did not follow the true path. In the 20th century, movie depiction of werewolves, such as Lon Chaney Jnr's genre-defining version in the 1941 film, *The Wolf Man*, in which he is seen as a lonely, tortured outsider who has accidentally become a werewolf, changed people's perceptions. Nowadays, werewolf characters are often the sympathetic he-roes, fighting against evil or trying to live a normal life despite the difficulties they encounter whenever the moon is full.

In ancient times, there were many stories of men who turned into wolves, including Homer's depiction in the *Odyssey* of the creatures that the magical and beautiful Circe had enchanted and made into werewolves and were-lions. Even Odysseus's men fell for her tricks and became were-swine. But it was in medieval romances - the heroic literature of chivalry popular in aristocratic circles in High Medieval and Early Modern Europe - that werewolves first began to appear. Until around 1600, these fantastic tales of the adventures of kings, princes, knights and nobles, of dragons and damsels in distress - and, occasionally, werewolves - were immensely popular, the bestsellers of their day.

DER WÄRWOLF

DIVEKY
ZÜRICH
1911

The Werewolf, postcard by the Viennese Werkstaette.
Colour Lithographie by Josef von Diveky, 1911.

The romances of *Bisclavret* and *Guillaume de Palerme* (see pages 64-5), depict the werewolf as benign, a victim of circumstance, wronged by wicked magic and knights errant with evil intent. In folklore, however, the werewolf was anything but benign. Medieval theology had something to do with this depiction, of course, men of religion desirous of a population that was fully aware of the consequences of straying towards the supernatural. Therefore, the werewolf is shown as a human being who has gone wrong and has made a pact with the devil, becoming his servant and carrying out his orders. The taboo of cannibalism - perhaps the most extreme of all - is breached by such creatures, creating intense loathing and disgust in the population at large.

SEXUAL THEMES

From the beginning, sexual themes are often to be found in werewolf fiction. In the film *Werewolf of London*, the protagonist murders his girlfriend out of sexual jealousy as she strolls with a former lover. *An American Werewolf in London* features a love affair between David, the American of the title and a nurse called Alex that he falls in love with and Michael Jackson's *Thriller* video is set against the backdrop of the singer walking his girlfriend home and placing a ring on her finger to symbolize that they are going steady.

The fairy tale *Little Red Riding Hood* (see page 132), is notoriously replete with Freudian imagery and allegory. There are countless layers of meaning to this tale, from the simple story of the consequences of not doing as you are told to the symbolic weight of the experience of life, symbolized

by the rocks that Little Red Riding Hood places inside the wolf before sewing him back up again. Angela Carter's novel *The Company of Wolves* and the movie *Ginger Snaps*, as well as many other fictional depictions of werewolves, owe a great deal to this simple fairy tale.

GOTHIC HORROR

The explosion of Gothic horror novels in the 19th century provided plenty of opportunities for the werewolf legend to be re-visited. A genre that blended horror and romance was invented in 1764 by Horace Walpole with his novel *The Castle of Otranto* and its blend of melodrama and parody created a pleasing type of terror that was coloured greatly by the Romantic literary style that was a fairly new phenomenon when Walpole was writing. Werewolves were amongst the fantastic cast of characters of this genre that also included magicians, vampires, monsters (such as Frankenstein's monster, created by Mary Shelley), demons, dragons and angels.

G.W.M. Reynolds' 1847 Gothic novel, *Wagner the Wehr-Wolf*, was a typical example of the genre, a tale of a German peasant who has made a deal with the devil to turn into a murderous werewolf every seven years in return for a good life. The transformation of the protagonist Wagner represents the good and evil sides of the personality, the wolf form showing the evil, dark nature that we all possess.

The 20th century brought countless werewolf books, stories and films. Amongst the specialists of the genre was the great supernatural storyteller Algernon Blackwood who featured werewolves in a number of his works. And the growth of the comic maga-

Coloured woodcut, 1893, used to illustrate
Little Red Riding Hood, The Brothers Grimm.

zine in the United States from the 1920s to the 1950s provided another medium for such work, especially in such titles as *Weird Tales* for which writers such as H. Warner Munn, Seabury Quinn and Manley Wade Wellman provided wonderfully gruesome stories.

In 1933, American author, Guy Endore published *The Werewolf of Paris*, a novel that many have considered the werewolf equivalent to Bram Stoker's *Dracula*. Ham-

mer Films produced an adaptation of it in 1961's *The Curse of the Werewolf*. The 1935 film *Werewolf of London* added a new twist to the werewolf legend on film, the first to depict an anthropomorphic werewolf. This brought humanity to the creature and induced sympathy in the audience. It also introduced to werewolf films the motif of the werewolf always killing the thing he loved most.

THE CLASSIC MOVIE WEREWOLF

This new style werewolf was rounded out as a full-blown character with whom we could engage in Lon Chaney Jnr's depiction of *The Wolf Man* in Universal Pictures' 1941 release. Now lycanthropy was being shown entirely as a curse or a disease and we sympathized completely with the sufferer's plight. Interestingly, the werewolf's character, no matter how gentle or good he is in human form, remains cunning, callous and bloodthirsty after he undergoes the painful - it is always a painful experience on film - transformation to lupine form.

The greatest of all film werewolves, Lon Chaney Jnr returned in the role several times and in his films some elements of standard werewolf lore are firmly established - the full moon transformation of *Frankenstein Meets the Wolf Man* of 1943 and silver bullets as the only means of killing a werewolf in *House of Frankenstein* of 1944. He also appeared as the Wolf Man in 1945's *House of Dracula* and the parodic *Abbot and Costello Meet Frankenstein*. After a quick break, werewolf movies suddenly came to the fore again in 1981 with two hugely successful productions - *An American Werewolf in London* and *The Howling*.

THE CONTEMPORARY BEAST

The modern werewolf has associations far removed from the depictions of the past. Issues such as environmentalism have suggested the werewolf as a symbol of a humanity more in tune with nature. The role-playing game *Werewolf: The Apocalypse* allows players to assume the roles of werewolves, Garoux, who are on the side of a force known as Gaia, against the destructive supernatural spirit, the Wyrm, a symbol of industrialization and industrial pollution.

The ever-popular *Dr. Who* and the *Harry Potter* novels have featured werewolves, the latter depicting one teacher, Remus Lupin, as a werewolf terrified of spreading his infection. In the *Harry Potter* series, however, although werewolves are shown as a threat, they are also shown as symbolizing marginalized groups who have been victimized or discriminated against. Today it is popular to show werewolves in fiction as a separate species or race. Sometimes, too, people are depicted with special powers or magic that enables them to transform into werewolves at will. In such fiction, they become werewolves either through birth or by being bitten by a werewolf.

Portrait of Oliver Reed as Leon Corledo in *The Curse of the Werewolf*, Terence Fisher, 1961.

LITTLE RED RIDING HOOD

The fairy tale *Little Red Riding Hood* is probably the best-known of all werewolf stories. Admittedly, the creature in the story is always described as a 'Big Bad' wolf, but it talks and has human attributes that tell us that this is no mere wolf. The story can be traced back to oral versions that originate in several European countries probably before the 17th century. French peasants told the tale in the 14th century and it was also told around that time in Italy in a number of different versions.

Its conscious or unconscious association with werewolves is ever present. In fact, a version of the tale called *The Story of a Grandmother* collected in 1870, although it is without doubt much older, describes the villain of the piece as a *bzou*, which is another name for werewolf. It probably reflects the werewolf hysteria that existed in medieval times. The full horror of the werewolf trials, such as those of the German serial killer, Peter Stubbe, are illustrated in versions of the narrative in which the wolf serves up the grandmother's flesh to the little girl.

SEXUAL CONNOTATIONS

It was first published by Charles Perrault in Paris in 1697. Already the sexual connotations often ascribed to the story are apparent in one of the illustrations that accompanied it. It showed the wolf climbing into bed on top of the girl. French slang of the time for a girl having lost her virginity was to have 'seen the wolf'. Another interpretation of the tale is about sexual awakening - the red cloak symbolizes the menstrual cycle, the dark forest represents womanhood and the wolf symbolizes a man who could be a lover, seducer or sexual predator.

The tale has been told and retold for years in various mediums. In 2011 it reached the big screen in the form of American horror film *Red Riding Hood*. In this adaptation of the story, from *Twilight* director Catherine Hardwicke, a remote village is tormented by a werewolf. It is set in the middle ages and focuses on Valerie (Amanda Seyfried), who is betrothed to a wealthy man named Henry (Jeremy Irons) but is secretly in love with Peter (Shiloh Fernandez). The couple decide to run away so they can stay together and are about to leave when they discover that Valerie's sister has been killed by the werewolf. Until this point the creature has been kept at bay by the villagers offering it a monthly animal sacrifice. But this time, and under a blood red moon, the werewolf has craved human meat. The villagers enlist the help of werewolf hunter Father Solomon (Gary Oldman) who brings with him the knowledge that the werewolf takes human form by day, leading the community to grow suspicious of each other. As the hysteria spreads, Valerie tries to uncover the true identity of the beast, drawing herself closer to danger.

At its greatest, *Little Red Riding Hood* is simply one of the best werewolf stories of all, proven by its endurance through the centuries and by its hidden messages which continue to teach and entertain.

Scene still from *Red Riding Hood*,
Catherine Hardwicke, 2011.

THE STRANGE CASE OF
DR JEKYLL
& MR HYDE
ROBERT LOUIS STEVENSON (1886)

The werewolf myth is, of course, often described as a metaphor for the duality of human nature, the struggle that is waged within each of us between good and evil. Charles Darwin theorized that, having evolved from the ape, man has an animalistic side to him that is restrained in a delicate balance only by morality and the strictures of modern society. In his 1886 novel, *The Strange Case of Dr Jekyll and Mr Hyde*, Robert Louis Stevenson explores our innate duality, the characters of the title becoming metaphors for the two sides of human nature.

Dr Henry Jekyll's life has been a struggle between good and evil, a struggle that has resulted in him isolating himself from people who care about him. The potion he creates turns him into the younger, but cruel and remorseless Mr Edward Hyde who is the evil side of Jekyll's personality made repulsively manifest, a killer who becomes increasingly more difficult to control. Eventually, as Hyde grows stronger Jekyll finds that he has trouble remaining himself.

The story begins one Sunday, as a prominent London lawyer, Gabriel John Utterson and his friend and distant relative, Richard Enfield, take a walk through London. Enfield tells his companion about an odd encounter he had recently. Whilst returning home late one night, he saw an unpleasant-looking man trampling a small, screaming girl. When a crowd gathered, the man, Hyde, had disappeared through a door at the rear of a house owned by Jekyll and returned with £100 to pay off the girl's family. Part of the payment was in the form of a cheque signed by Jekyll.

'Unscientific Balderdash'

Jekyll is actually a client of Utterson and he learns that the doctor has written a will in which he has left all of his money and property to Hyde. Puzzled, Utterson decides to investigate further, staking out the door in Jekyll's house through which Hyde had gone to get the money to pay the girl's

THE FEATURES SEEMED TO MELT AND ALTER

Illustration showing Dr Jekyll's transformation. From
the novel *The Strange Case of Dr Jekyll and Mr Hyde*,
Robert Louis Stevenson, 1886.

parents. After a considerable wait, he sees Hyde approach the door and engages him in conversation. Hyde, becoming suspicious of Utterson's questions, hurries into the house. Knocking at the front door of the house, Utterson is informed by Jekyll's butler, Poole, that Hyde has complete access to the house. Curious, Utterson consults a friend who also knows Jekyll. Dr Hastie Lanyon tells him that he had fallen out with Jekyll years previously following a dispute over Jekyll's research, which is described by Lanyon as 'unscientific balderdash'. But several weeks later, Utterson has the opportunity to question Jekyll himself about the mysterious Hyde when he is invited to a dinner party at his house. Jekyll is unhappy with Utterson's questioning, however, and merely reiterates testily that Hyde is to be his beneficiary on his death.

A year later, a distinguished elderly man, Sir Danvers Carew, a Member of Parliament, is found murdered and, although his assailant has escaped before he can be apprehended, a maid identifies him as Hyde. When Utterson and the police arrive at Hyde's apartment, they discover from the housekeeper that he has fled. They immediately seek out Jekyll who shows them a letter from Hyde stating that he was going to disappear forever. For his part, Jekyll insists that he wants nothing more to do with him.

A Mysterious Envelope

Jekyll seems to change with the disappearance of Hyde, becoming more approachable and sociable. Meanwhile, Lanyon dies suddenly, leaving an envelope addressed to Utterson. Inside is a mysterious sealed envelope with instructions that it is not to be opened until either the death or disappearance of Jekyll. Utterson cannot help thinking that it contains information about Hyde.

Utterson and Enfield still take their customary Sunday constitutional and on one of these, as they pass Jekyll's house, they look up, catching sight of him at the window. They invite him to join them on their walk, but the doctor appears to be afraid or in terrible pain and turns away from the window. Utterson and Enfield are distressed by the experience.

A little later, Utterson receives a visit at his house by Jekyll's servant, Poole, who expresses concern about his master. He tells Utterson that Jekyll has not left his laboratory for the past week and had sent him on trips to numerous chemists in a frantic search for a mysterious drug. Poole insisted to the lawyer that Jekyll had been murdered as the voice he heard from within the lab was not that of his master. The killer, he insisted, must therefore still be inside the laboratory. Utterson agrees to return to the house with the servant to investigate and on arriving, the two men break down the locked door of the laboratory. To their horror, they find that the mysterious man Poole had mentioned has just killed himself by drinking poison. Before them lies the body of Hyde, dressed in Jekyll's clothes. They search the house for Jekyll but there is no sign of him. They do, however, come upon a note addressed to Utterson. It instructs him to return to his house and read the letter in the sealed envelope that has been left to him by Lanyon. It turns out to be the 'confession' of Jekyll.

Lanyon writes that Jekyll had written to him and requested him to carefully follow the instructions he provided. He was instructed to go to Jekyll's laboratory and find the items that were listed in the letter

and take them back to his house. At midnight, someone whom Lanyon would not know would call at the house for the items. Sure enough, Lanyon goes on, a repulsive individual had knocked at the door on the stroke of midnight, stating that he was there to claim the things that Jekyll had asked Lanyon to remove from his laboratory. The man asked for a 'graduated glass' and swiftly poured the liquids and powders into it. He had then drunk the resulting potion. Lanyon was horrified by the sight that then unfolded in front of him - the hideous creature began to transform into his former friend, Jekyll. Lanyon ends the letter by informing Utterson that the man who had arrived at his door at midnight was none other than Hyde.

A Double Life

In the second letter Jekyll explains how he had led a double life and had committed some acts of which he was ashamed. He had decided to investigate the scientific possibilities of separating his good side from his darker side and through his research, discovered a means of transforming himself into a creature that was completely free of the constraints of conscience, Hyde. However, second personality he had created was evil and, in fact, his own identity was still far from the embodiment of good. He had become concerned when he found himself transforming into Hyde involuntarily and determined to stop his experiments. One night, however, the urge seized him once more and he murdered Sir Danvers Carew.

An End to the Madness

Again, he writes, he resolved to stop the transformations, immersing himself in philanthropic work that he believed had redeemed him. However, the involuntary nature of his transformations became worse and he had found himself needing Lanyon's help in returning to his Jekyll self. The potion had begun to run out and he had found himself unable to make more as the secret lay in an impurity in the first batch that he would never be able to replicate. Faced with having to live his life as Hyde, he had decided to commit suicide.

The Strange Case of Dr Jekyll and Mr Hyde stands with Bram Stoker's *Dracula* (1897) and Mary Shelley's *Frankenstein* as one of the great works of Gothic horror and its abiding popularity can be seen, as with those works, in the number of adaptations - film, stage and television - that have been made. Its influence has been immense, including such fantastic characters as The Hulk, Two-Face and countless other shapeshifting comic book superheroes.

IT CHILLS YOU!
HALF-MAN!
HALF-MONSTER!
M-G-M'S
ALL-TIME
GREAT
Screen Play by JOHN LEE MAHIN

OM M·G·M's HALL OF FAME

PENCER TRACY

NGRID   LANA
RGMAN · TURNER

ICTOR FLEMING'S production of

ll and Mr. Hyde
with DONALD CRISP

EL BY
EVENSON · Directed by VICTOR FLEM

Film poster for *Dr Jekyll and Mr Hyde*, Victor Fleming, 1941.

STEPPENWOLF
HERMAN HESSE (1926)

In 1924, while living in Basel, the German writer Herman Hesse left behind the problems of his unstable marriage and moved into an apartment. Depressed by his failure to make his marriage work, he found himself becoming increasingly lonely and isolated from his fellow human beings, feelings that resulted in him even contemplating suicide. Out of this experience emerged the novel *Steppenwolf*, in which he vented his feelings of isolation and in which he saw himself as an outsider, like the wolf that roams the grassy plains of the European steppes.

In the book, Harry Haller - the 'Steppenwolf' of the title - leaves a manuscript behind in a boarding house. The landlady's nephew discovers the manuscript and publishes it. The manuscript's first section deals with the background to the story, the protagonist describing his intellectual aloofness, his contempt for what he sees as a narrow-minded and vacuous bourgeois society and his inability to mix with others. Steppenwolf, however, is not only separated by his elitist nature, but also by what he believes to be his dual nature - part human and part wolf. He sees his inner conflict as a battle between the man in him - high and intellectual - and the wolf in him - low and animalistic. He longs to live like a wolf, liberated from social convention and the demands of society, but is forced to live the life of a bourgeois bachelor and in order to avoid the stigma of being diagnosed as

a 'schizomaniac', must conceal this part of himself. As a consequence, he finds himself increasingly isolated from others. Of course, this isolation suits him, but it is also destructive and he is aware that it could lead to insanity. Nonetheless, he also retains some humanity and 'wished, as every sentient being does, to be loved as a whole'. Death is, of course, an option, but Harry finds the idea of suicide abhorrent.

Wolverine Hallucinations

Harry meets a hedonistic young woman, Hermine, who introduces him to the indulgences of the bourgeoisie, teaching him about physical sensation and pleasures, including dancing and drugs. He is exposed to a number of physical experiences that are designed by her to draw out his multiple selves. As a result, Harry's devastating isolation begins to diminish and he forms a

closer bond to Hermine. But eventually in the Magic Theatre - a place where Harry experiences the fantasies that exist only in his mind - he murders her while seeing himself as a wolf.

In the late 1960s, no hippie's bookshelf was complete without *Steppenwolf*, the story - part autobiography and part fantasy - encapsulates a number of critical elements of the sixties hipster make-up - sex, drugs and Buddhism. This was especially true of the

section that deals with the 'magic theatre', interpreted by many as psychedelic in nature and approximating the experience achieved by taking LSD. *Steppenwolf*, therefore, became a fixture of sixties popular culture. The influential San Francisco Magic Theatre Company borrowed its name from the book and the rock band Steppenwolf, formed in 1967 by German-born John Kay, enjoyed massive worldwide success with the appropriately named single *Born to Be Wild*.

Herman Hesse, author of *Steppenwolf*.

THE CALL OF THE WILD AND WHITE FANG

JACK LONDON (1903 & 1906)

In the early 1900s, American writer Jack London wrote two books about dogs and their relationship with the wolf inside them that remain hugely popular to this day – *The Call of the Wild* and *White Fang*. The books mirror each other, in *The Call of the Wild*, the canine protagonist makes a journey from domesticity to life in the wild, while the eponymous *White Fang* reverses that journey, migrating from life as a wolfdog to an existence of comfortable domesticity.

THE CALL OF THE WILD

Buck is a four-year-old half St Bernard and half Scottish sheepdog, living in the Santa Clara home of Judge Miller. Around this time, however, gold is discovered in Canada's Yukon Territory and large dogs, useful for pulling sleds, become particularly prized. Buck is stolen for this purpose, suffering beatings and mistreatment as he is taken north where he has to quickly learn to become a member of a sled team. He also has to learn how to survive in the harsh conditions of the Yukon but begins to discover the primordial instinct that has lain dormant within him during his life of comfortable domesticity. This new-found strength enables him to defeat his mortal enemy, Spitz, lead dog of his team, in a vicious fight, and usurp his position.

The Song of the Pack

Buck falls into the hands of three amateur adventurers who set out on an ill-advised trek into the wilderness. By the time they arrive at a frozen river, however, they have run out of food and Buck refuses to go on. He is rescued from the subsequent beating by a man named John Thornton who warns the three of the perils of continuing with their journey. They stubbornly refuse, and Buck and Thornton watch as they disappear with their sled beneath the treacherously thin ice. While Thornton looks for gold, Buck fills his time with trips into the wilderness where he befriends and runs with wolves. Returning to camp one day, he discovers that his owner has been murdered by Yeehat Indians. He exacts revenge on Thornton's

killers but with his ties to civilization now finally severed, he answers the call of the wild, joining the wolves and singing 'the song of the pack'.

WHITE FANG

White Fang is a three-quarters wolf-dog hybrid who is born in the wild. He and his mother get adopted by some Native Americans, after one of them, Grey Beaver, recognizes White Fang's mother as Kiche, his brother's wolfdog. He christens the cub White Fang, but in the Indian camp, life is harsh for the young dog. The camp dogs are unfriendly towards him and he learns that in order to survive, he must become superior to them in every way. To this end, he turns himself into a savage and indomitable fighter.

Dog-fighting

At the age of five, he is traded for a bottle of whiskey to a dog-fighter and begins a successful career as a fighter. One day it seems as if he has met his match when he is pitted against a savage bulldog. Just as it seems he is going to be killed by his opponent, he is rescued by a young gold prospector, Weedon Scott. White Fang returns to California with Scott, but faces one more battle when he kills a man who tries to kill his master,

now a judge. The women of the estate on which he lives fondly name him 'The Blessed Wolf' as a result, and the novel ends with the formerly wild White Fang lying in the sun in Santa Clara, the pups he has fathered with the sheepdog Collie playing happily around him.

Both books serve as a reminder of how close we all are to encountering the wolf inside each of us and how little it would take to return us to the wild that is always calling us.

Front cover of Jack London's *White Fang*, 1906.

OTHER WEREWOLF STORIES

HUGUES, THE WER-WOLF
Sutherland Menzies (1838)

The Gothic horror story that became hugely popular in the 19th century drew on folklore and legend and presented it in a new fictional form. *Hugues, the Wer-Wolf* is an early example and is probably the first known werewolf story. Set in the English county of Kent, it utilizes the now-familiar motif of the werewolf's paw being cut off, leaving its human form without a hand after he has returned to that form.

THE PHANTOM SHIP
Frederick Maryatt (1839)

A Gothic novel that explores the legend of the *Flying Dutchman*. Earthly and unearthly powers appear and in chapter two a demonic femme fatale transforms from woman to wolf.

WAGNER THE WEHR-WOLF
G.M.W. Reynolds (1847)

Another Gothic horror story, *Wagner* portrays the classic werewolf story of a cursed man who is transformed into a werewolf at the time of the full moon. His werewolf side represents the dark side of man's dual nature, the evil, wicked side that lusts after blood.

THE WOLF LEADER
(Le Meneur de Loups)
Alexandre Dumas (1857)

A fantasy novel by the great French author, based on a local folk tale Dumas heard when he was a child, it tells the story of a cobbler, Thibault, who takes the offer of becoming a werewolf in order to wreak revenge on his enemies.

THE WERE-WOLF
Clemence Houseman (1896)

A seductive femme fatale transforms into a werewolf and devours her unfortunate male suitors in this work, acclaimed as one of the best werewolf stories.

RUNNING WOLF
Algernon Blackwood (1921)

A beautiful story featuring a benign were-wolf who, after initially appearing to be sinister, emerges as friendly and surprisingly human.

THE UNDYING MONSTER
Jessie Douglas Kerruish (1922)

For centuries, the Hammond family has suffered from a werewolf curse. When family members begin to fall prey to wolf attacks, a police detective investigates and discovers that the curse has returned once again.

DARKER THAN YOU THINK
Jack Williamson (1940)

An ethnological expedition to Mongolia discovers that there are people who can turn themselves into animals. A murder in the camp leads to the discovery that in times past a war was fought between Homo sapiens and werewolves, the former winning. However, the werewolves live on hidden in the forms of humans awaiting the Child of the Night who will lead them to victory.

Illustration from *Wagner the Wehr-Wolf*, G.M.W. Reynolds, 1847.

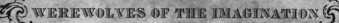

THERE SHALL BE NO DARKNESS
James Blish (1950)

A group of people in a remote country manor learn that one amongst them is a werewolf. It attempts a scientific explanation for werewolfism when one character describes it as the result of a mutation in the pineal gland of the afflicted person's brain.

THREE HEARTS AND THREE LIONS
Poul Anderson (1961)

Following an explosion during World War II, Holger Carlsen is transported to a parallel world set in French medieval history. He learns that he has been sent there to fight the evil of Faerie and amongst his enemies are werewolves. The novel influenced the game *Dungeons & Dragons*.

OPERATION CHAOS
Poul Anderson (1971)

A fantasy novel set in an alternative world in which the existence of God has been scientifically proven and magic has been harnessed for practical use. Werewolf Steven Matuchek and witch Virginia are on a mission to stop an invading Islamic army from unleashing a superweapon, a genie that was sealed in a bottle by King Solomon.

THE WOLFEN
Whitley Strieber (1978)

Two New York police detectives discover that a pack of intelligent and savage wolf-like creatures are stalking the streets of the city, hunting the homeless, the drug abusers and outcasts.

THE TALISMAN
Stephen King and Peter Straub (1983)

A re-working of the Walter Scott novel of the same name, following the adventures of a 12-year-old boy, Jack Sawyer, who becomes involved with a parallel world called 'the Territories' after finding an enchanted crystal called 'the Talisman'.

CYCLE OF THE WEREWOLF
Stephen King (1985)

A short horror novel by the master storyteller, featuring a werewolf that is killing people and doing dark deeds every full moon in a small Maine town. In the same year of publication, this book was turned into a film called *Silver Bullet*. It has since come to be regarded by fans of the werewolf genre as one of the best werewolf movies ever made.

THE WOLF'S HOUR
Robert R. McCammon (1989)

A World War II adventure novel with a twist - the British agent sent behind German lines to prevent a secret Nazi weapon being launched is in fact a werewolf.

THE DISCWORLD SERIES
Terry Pratchet (1983–)

The best-selling comedy fantasy book series, set on the Discworld, a flat world balanced on the backs of four elephants which stand on the back of a giant turtle. One of the members of the Ankh-Morpok City Watch, Captain Delphine Angua von Überwald, is in fact, from a family of werewolves. Angua rebels against the traditional werewolf lifestyle of her parents and brother and leaves Überwald to join the City Watch.

THE WEREWOLF'S KISS
Cheri Scotch (1992)

The first book in a trilogy about a pack of werewolves in New Orleans. Subsequent titles are *The Werewolf's Touch* (1993) and *The Werwewolf's Sin* (1994).

BLOOD TRAIL
Tanya Huff (1992)

This is the second in a series of six novels about a vampire who is on the trail of an assassin intent on wiping out Canada's last werewolf clan.

BLOOD AND CHOCOLATE
Annette Curtis Klause (1997)

A romantic supernatural werewolf novel for young adult readers, *Blood and Chocolate* features the *loups-garoux*, a separate species from humans. Vivian Gandillon loves changing from girl to wolf, but longs for a normal life. Then she falls in love with a human, a boy called Aiden, and a brutal murder threatens to expose her pack.

BITTEN
Kelley Armstrong (2001)

The first book in the *Women of the Otherworld* series, this fantasy novel features Elena Michaels who is tired of being the only female werewolf. She has left her pack and is living as a human in Toronto but when her pack leader asks for her help against a sudden uprising, she agrees to come to their aid. Once this is over, she will have repaid the pack and be free to get on with her human life.

Front cover of Steven King's
Cycle of the Werewolf, 1985.

NAKED BRUNCH
Sparkle Hayter (2003)

A comic novel featuring a girl finding her way in the big city. The trouble begins when she discovers she's a werewolf.

HUNTER'S MOON
Cathy Clamp and C.T. Adams (2004)

A novel of suspense and romance about a Mafia hitman who is also a werewolf. A 2005 sequel *Moon's Web*, continued the story and subsequent books featured more shape-shifters.

KITTY AND THE MIDNIGHT HOUR
Carrie Vaughn (2005)

The first of a modern take on werewolves featuring a young female werewolf who brings the existence of beings with 'paranatural biology' to the attention of the world. Other titles in the series are *Kitty Goes to Washington* (2006); *Kitty Takes a Holiday* (2007); *Kitty and the Silver Bullet* (2008); *Kitty and the Dead Man's Hand* (2009); and *Kitty Raises Hell* (2009).

LONELY WEREWOLF GIRL
Martin Millar (2007)

Werewolf Kalix MacRinnach is on the run in the streets of London, pursued by hunters who want to kill her. Meanwhile, in the Highlands of Scotland, the Clan MacRinnach has decided that she should be the next clan leader. The trouble is that she is on the run because she was the reason the previous clan chieftain died.

ANITA BLAKE: VAMPIRE HUNTER
Laurell K. Hamilton (1993–2000s)

The multi-volume best-selling *Anita Blake: Vampire Hunter* novels feature a heroine who is a legal vampire executioner and US Marshal. Various types of shapeshifters, including werewolves and were-rats appear and a distinction is made between lycanthropes, which include solely persons infected by contact with another lycanthrope's bodily fluids, and shapeshifters, a class that includes both lycanthropes and persons who are able to shapeshift as a result of magic, such as a personal or family curse.

RAISED BY WOLVES
Jennifer Lynn Barnes (2010)

Tough heroine Bryn is brought up by a pack of werewolves after her parents are murdered by a rabid werewolf. However, the pack has been keeping a secret and Bryn needs answers.

LONELY WERE WOLF GIRL

uite simply, the most compelling werewolf book o

MELISSA MARR

SHE DOESN'T
NEED ANYONE
OR ANYTHING
- BUT THEY ALL
WANT HER

Raised
by
Wolves

Jennifer Lynn Barnes

Front covers of Martin Millar's *Lonely Werewolf Girl*, 2007
and Jennifer Lynn Barnes's *Raised By Wolves*, 2010.

THE WOLF MAN
(1941)

In 1941, Universal Pictures released the last of their truly great monster movies, *The Wolf Man*. It had been 10 years since their last greatest hit *Dracula*, and in the interim period, Bela Lugosi, the vampire star of *Dracula*, had experienced a severe career decline and was no longer a box office attraction. Lon Chaney Jr, after acclaimed success in John Steinbeck's *Of Mice and Men* got the job. It was a role that would make him famous - Larry Talbot, The Wolf Man.

The film may have been low budget, but it was certainly not low quality. The cast was full of Oscar winners and nominees like Claude Rains, highly respected actors like Maria Ouspenskaya, and horror veterans like Ralph Bellamy and Bela Lugosi. The cinematography and score were both some of the finest in any of the Universal monster movies. The werewolf concepts invented by Curt Siodmak for the filmscript are legendary. The full moon, the werewolf's vulnerability to silver and the idea that in human form he is a decent fellow who just can't help his evil urges during transformation are all now standard werewolf characteristics.

The setting of the film is a British village. Production took place over three weeks in November 1941 and was completed a matter of days before the Japanese attack on Pearl Harbor, which brought America into World War II. The fictional horrors of *The Wolf Man* were intended as a welcome distraction to the real horrors of World War II.

Portrait of Lon Chaney Jr. as Wolf Man in *The Wolf Man*, George Waggner, 1941.

The story opens, with Larry Talbot (Lon Chaney Jr), second son of Sir John Talbot (Claude Rains) returning to the village of his birth to claim his right as heir to the Talbot fortune and title. Larry had left home to find his own way in America for 17 years as his older brother was being groomed to become Lord Talbot. A hunting accident ended his brother's life, making Larry the next in line. Larry and his father pledge to let their strained relationship be buried in the past and they forge a new, closer father-son bond.

Almost immediately on his return, Larry falls for Gwen Conliffe (Evelyn Ankers) the daughter of the village antiques dealer. Chaney and Ankers appeared in many more films together after *The Wolf Man*, their sizzling celluloid chemistry being a complete contrast to their frosty offscreen relationship.

Larry accompanies Gwen and her friend Jenny to a gypsy camp in the woods to have their fortunes told. Jenny is separated from her friends and is attacked in the misty woods by a rabid werewolf. Larry hears Jenny's cries and runs to her aid, in the course of trying to rescue her and killing the creature however, he is bitten by the werewolf. Maleva, the wrinkled and ancient gypsy dispenses her prediction that anyone bitten by a werewolf will turn into a werewolf too. Her words foretelling Larry's transformation into the new killer werewolf of the woods.

The theme of the beast within the man is strong in this *Jekyll and Hyde* retelling. While Robert Louis Stevenson's Mr Hyde is not technically a werewolf, his alter ego Dr Jekyll definitely shapeshifts between man and psychopath, good and evil, love and resentment, tenderness and violence. All these also throb beneath the troubled skin of Larry Talbot in an expression of the 'primitive duality of man' - we all have our dark side but most of us manage to keep it under control, although occasionally it does break out.

By modern standards the make-up for *The Wolf Man* is laughable with Lon Chaney Jr looking more like a giant rat than a wolf. But make-up magician Jack Pierce who was also responsible for *Frankenstein* and many other Universal Pictures monsters, was working with primitive materials like yak hair, glue and cotton. There were no computer graphics or animatronics in 1941. Censors at the time also prevented the Wolf Man from looking too scary, nor would they allow direct man-to-beast transformations. Curiously enough, that did work out better in the end, saving the studio money, and holding back the big metamorphosis scene for the climax of the movie when Larry Talbot transforms back from wolf to man. (Larry miraculously did not die, however, and went on to appear in four more films.)

In 2010 a remake of *The Wolf Man* was released. Starring popular actors such as Benico del Toro and Antony Hopkins, and with modern technology at the film-makers disposal, it seemed guaranteed to be a hit. However, at the box office it was a flop, later finding some popularity when released on DVD. Critics compared the two films and the 1941 version came out on top, proving that despite all cinema can achieve now, it couldn't quite recreate the charm of the original. *The Wolf Man* is truly one of the greatest horror films of the ages, ranking alongside *Dracula* and *Frankenstein* as foundation stones upon which all modern horror movie archetypes are based. But while the make-up and sets may be part of the annals of cinema history, the story and acting is as compelling today as it was in 1941.

Film poster for *The Wolf Man*, George Waggner, 1941.

AN AMERICAN WEREWOLF IN LONDON
(1981)

This film follows the journey of two American friends as they embark on a backpacking tour of England. Jack and David are exploring the Yorkshire Moors when they come across a country pub, rather ominously called The Slaughtered Lamb. The two men go in for a drink and to book a room for the night. Jack notices a pentagram on the wall, a sign often associated with paganism. He asks what it is, and the pub falls silent. They start to feel uneasy so they decide to leave, and the locals offer advice such as, 'keep to the roads', and, bizarrely, 'beware the full moon'. These warnings should have been enough to convince them to stay, but they leave, and before they know it they have forgotten the advice and find themselves lost on the moors, as a full moon is uncovered by the clouds. Back at the pub, the owner becomes concerned, and asks the patrons whether they ought to go after the pair. But, as the sound of howling can be heard in the distance, the locals barricade themselves in the pub, leaving David and Jack to fend for themselves. On the Moors, the duo have also heard the howling of a wolf, and before they know it they are faced with a monstrous beast. The creature attacks the pair and succeeds in killing Jack, when suddenly the locals emerge, and shoot it down. The next thing David knows, he is in a London hospital. It has been three weeks since the attack and he gets told that Jack has died. When the police arrive to take his statement he insists he was attacked by a large wolf, but the police think otherwise and blame an escaped lunatic. The film takes a stranger turn when through dream sequences we get an insight into David's mental state. Soon, David is visited by a dead Jack, who assures him they were attacked by a werewolf and as a result, David has become a werewolf too. Jack explains that in order to escape the same fate as himself, David must kill himself before the next full moon. This would also break the spell for Jack, who will remain in a zombie-like living dead state until the bloodline of the werewolf that attacked them has been stopped. Some time passes and David does not act on Jack's advice. Then one night, as Jack had predicted, a full moon shines in the night sky and David begins to feel excruciating pain. He transforms into a werewolf with lots of grey fur, a grotesque face and long sharp fangs. He runs rampant on the streets of London, and on the Underground system, killing six Londoners. The next thing he knows he is naked, in a wolf cage at London Zoo. Later, having escaped the zoo, David transforms again and goes on another killing spree, before being cornered by police and shot dead. *An American Werewolf in London* uses the creepy setting of the Yorkshire Moors coupled with England's connection with werewolf folklore to create a classic story about a terrifying beast that lurks in the woods.

Film poster for *An American Werewolf in London*
John Landis, 1981.

FROM THE DIRECTOR OF ANIMAL HOUSE...
A DIFFERENT KIND OF ANIMAL.
AN AMERICAN WEREWOLF
IN LONDON
THE MONSTER MOVIE
POLYGRAM PICTURES PRESENTS
A LYCANTHROPE FILMS LIMITED PRODUCTION
AN AMERICAN WEREWOLF IN LONDON
STARRING DAVID NAUGHTON, JENNY AGUTTER
GRIFFIN DUNNE & JOHN WOODVINE
ORIGINAL MUSIC BY ELMER BERNSTEIN
EXECUTIVE PRODUCERS PETER GUBER & JON PETERS
PRODUCED BY GEORGE FOLSEY, JR.
WRITTEN AND DIRECTED BY JOHN LANDIS

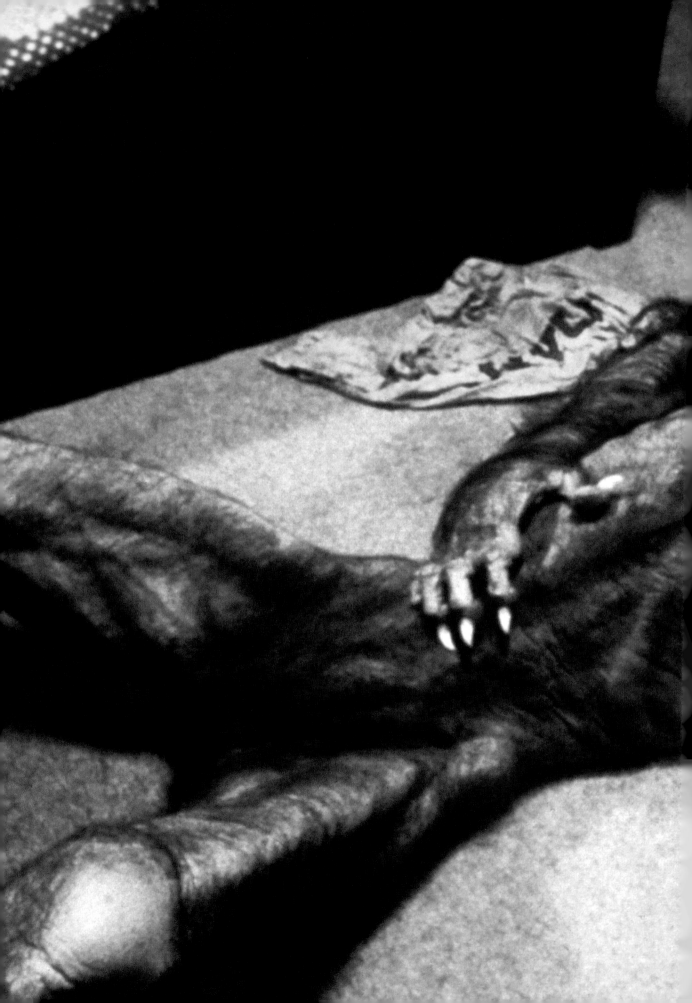

Scene still from *An American Werewolf in London*,
John Landis, 1981.

TEEN WOLF
(1985)

Teen Wolf is an American high school fantasy-comedy from the 1980s. It deals with two common themes typical of this era in film-making: adolescence and romance. The main character, Scott Howard (Michael J Fox), is sick of being average, and wishes there was something special about him. At the beginning of the film we see Scott playing basketball at high school against their rival team. He gets confronted on the basketball court by Mick, who happens to be the boyfriend of the girl he likes, Pamela. Mick and Scott are locked into a staring match, when Mick utters the word, 'dork'. Something inside Scott changes and he lets out an animal-like growl, causing Mick to drop the ball. Throughout the game Scott notices that the squeaky sound of shoes on the gym floor has become deafening, and that's only the beginning of his peculiar symptoms. After the game he speaks to Pamela, and as he becomes nervous thick hair starts to appear on his hands, only to disappear after a few moments. Soon, a rash surfaces on his neck, and then when he tries to illegally purchase alcohol and the shopkeeper stops him, his eyes glow red and his voice takes on an otherworldly tone. The bizarre changes do not stop there. At a party he suffers from aches and pains, and starts to sweat profusely. Then, after a party game in which he is dared to go into a cupboard with his friend Boof for a few minutes, he comes out looking disheveled, and her clothes appear to have been torn by claws. Scott races home and locks himself in

the bathroom. He looks in the mirror and splashes cold water on his face. Suddenly, his fingernails start to grow, the bones in his face move, fangs shoot down from his gums, his ears become pointed and his voice changes. During his transformation, his dad knocks at the door. Scott, scared to show himself, asks his dad to go away, but he keeps knocking. Finally Scott opens the door and has the biggest shock of all: his dad is also a werewolf. Through the window we then see a full moon and hear howling in the distance.

The pair of werewolves sit down for a rather unusual father-son chat. His dad tries to persuade him that being a werewolf has awesome perks such as superhuman strength and razor-sharp senses. However Scott is not convinced, 'I can look forward to a life of stealing babies in the middle of the night. And killing chickens. Fearing full moons, dodging silver bullets.' To which his dad replies, 'don't believe everything you see in the movies... the werewolf is part of you, but that doesn't change the inside'.

When Scott goes to high school the next day and his condition overcomes him during a basketball game, the players and audience stare at him in fascination, unsure whether to be scared or accept him. After a long pause, the game resumes and the crowd excitedly cheer for him, growing more rapturous by the second. Due to the powers afforded to him by his hereditary werewolf gene, he is now the best basketball player the school has ever seen and Scott, now

known as The Wolf, plays an outstanding game, leading the team to success for the first time. He becomes immensely popular and soon feels more than average, but later realizes that this comes at a cost. *Teen Wolf* is an interesting werewolf movie as it doesn't represent Scott as a threatening character, in fact, the film rarely touches on the terrifying capabilities this teenage werewolf has. Instead, the werewolf inside Scott is a physical manifestation of how he wants to be seen, and arguably a metaphor for the confusing and conflicting mixture of feelings that teenagers develop and sometimes find hard to contain. *Teen Wolf* uses the myth in a comedic and light-hearted manner, paving the way for a sequel and spin-off TV show.

Film poster for *Teen Wolf*, Rod Daniel, 1985.

HARRY POTTER AND THE PRISONER OF AZKABAN

(2002)

Scene still from *Harry Potter and the Prisoner of Azkaban*, Alfonso Cuarón, 2004. Showing Professor Lupin (far background of photo) who transforms into a werewolf.

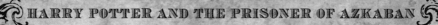

The third installment in the incredibly popular *Harry Potter* franchise, is the *Prisoner of Azkaban*. The werewolf myth is incorporated into this story, and it is expanded on with the creation of the Animagus.

In their Potions class, Professor Snape shows his pupils slides of ancient werewolves devouring people, and asks them the difference between an Animagus and a werewolf. The young witches and wizards fall silent and Hermione, the class boffin, puts her hand up, desperate to answer his question. She explains that:

> An Animagus is a wizard who elects to turn into an animal. A werewolf has no choice in the matter. Furthermore, the werewolf actively hunts humans and responds only to the call of its own kind.

Her answer is correct, and it is met by the obnoxious Draco Malfoy howling like a wolf to the delight of his idiotic friends. At this point in the story, Hermione hasn't told anyone that she suspects one of her teachers to be a werewolf.

Defence Against the Dark Arts Professor Remus Lupin has a dark secret, and the clue is in his surname. In a key scene in the story, Hermione's suspicions are confirmed when Lupin stands in the glare of the full moon and begins to transform

before her, Harry, Ron, Peter and Sirius. He stops dead in his tracks, and the camera zooms to capture the change in Lupin's face. Colour drains from his face, his eyes become bloodshot, changing quickly from blue to green and then his pupils dilate. His mouth opens and sharp fangs appear, pointed nails pierce through his fingertips and he screams as his body can no longer contain the beast within. His body begins to change shape, his clothes rip to reveal a curved spine, in seconds his feet become paws and he stands towering over his friends. His body no longer resembles a man, but a werewolf, as he shakes off his broken clothes and staggers about having lost any semblance of his human self. Hermione, Harry and Ron begin to edge away from the beast, but Hermione leans towards him and says, 'Professor?'. His eyes blaze and his long teeth glitter as he howls loudly at the moon. Snape appears and draws his wand, shielding the teenage trio, as the werewolf Lupin begins to pounce he is suddenly taken down midair by a giant dog. As the two animals hit the ground they fight ferociously and Harry sees the werewolf about to tear into the dog's neck. A howl is heard in the forest, and Lupin becomes momentarily distracted. Then a second howl is heard and he races off, leaving Harry to discover the dog was in fact Sirius Black, who had transformed into his Animagus form in order to protect the children. Later, it is revealed that Lupin is able to retain his human mind during transformations, as Professor Snape knew of Lupin's problem and provided him with a Wolfsbane potion. Unfortunately, he had not taken it that night, and so became a slave to the full moon that triggered his transformation.

DOG SOLDIERS
(2002)

British horror-comedy *Dog Soldiers* focuses on a band of soldiers that are sent to the Scottish Highlands on special training manoeuvres. The younger members of the group are especially annoyed to be out on an army exercise as they are missing the England -v- Germany World Cup qualifier. Little do they know that out in the woods there is something far more important to worry about. They are briefed on their mission and the men set out, armed with weaponry. After a short time they stop for a break, where their superior tells them about the remains of a young couple that were recently discovered by a park ranger, their tent ripped to shreds and blood everywhere. When night falls, a full moon appears in the sky and Special Operations Captain Ryan is out in the woods by himself. He hears something and looks through his night-vision goggles. He can't see anything near, and suddenly he is pounced on. The next day, the soldiers are walking through the woods when they stumble across pools of blood and guts. Captain Ryan emerges and says, 'help me', he looks to be in shock, and has a tear down his front with marks that seem to have been made by claws. Captain Ryan gives the soldiers only cryptic clues about what happened, but repeats a few times, 'there was only supposed to be one.' Soon, howling is heard as the soldiers run through the woods. The men are now being hunted by an unseen beast, which we soon discover to be a massive, ferocious werewolf. The monster stands tall, at least seven feet on its hind legs. It has a terrifying growl and sharp claws which tear through Sergeant Wells' abdomen, spilling his intestines out. The men are now together and being pursued by several werewolves, the men shooting constantly, trying to kill the beasts. In the distance a large car is seen, and one of the soldiers flags it down. Local zoologist Megan jumps out and screams at them all to get in. The men pile into the back and suddenly a werewolf is on the roof, shrieking and rocking the car. Its huge fangs are seen through the window and the men scream, the werewolf punches an arm through the roof, an arm which, though hairy, resembles that of a human. As Megan slams on the accelerator one of the soldiers grabs the werewolf's arm and hacks away at the hand with a knife, the car moving away before the soldier can grab his trophy. Megan and the men arrive at her place, and before long they realize that they are not in the company of nice people after all, but something far more sinister.

Scene still from *Dog Soldiers*, Neil Marshall, 2002.

Scene still from *Dog Soldiers*, Neil Marshall, 2002.

NEW MOON

(2009)

It could be argued that Stephenie Meyer's highly successful *Twilight* saga is responsible for refuelling the vampire craze in popular culture. Her novels cleverly mix romance with horror, capturing the imaginations of teenagers and adults alike. But there is another dark character that she has drawn out from the shadows: the werewolf, the age-old enemy of the vampire.

In his human form, Jacob Black is a Native American of the Quileute tribe (see page 88) in La Push, Forks, Washington. He befriends Bella Swan, who moves to Forks and quickly falls in love with local vampire Edward Cullen. As the story progresses, Bella comes to terms with Edward's affliction and is faced with the idea of becoming a vampire herself. Jacob is not a main character at this point, and he appears shy and awkward towards Bella. In the second book and film adaptation, *New Moon*, Jacob has come of age and the werewolf gene kicks in. He becomes very close to Bella when Edward leaves her, and his feelings begin to deepen. One day she is in the woods and confronted by Laurent, a vampire. The situation quickly spirals out of control and as she runs away, Jacob appears, coming to her rescue. As he runs towards the vampire he leaps into the air, transforming into a werewolf before he has hit the ground. Bella later becomes aware that Jacob's family descend from werewolves and that his tribe have a treaty with the Cullen family which exists to prevent vampires attacking humans. When Edward returns to Forks, Jacob reminds Edward of this treaty, emphasizing that Edward can never transform Bella into a vampire by biting her, as this will break the treaty and peace will cease to exist between the two supernatural forces.

The werewolves in the *Twilight* series are different from many other werewolf representations in literature and film. Their transformations are not triggered by the full moon, but when they need to defend themselves or protect others. They 'phase' into werewolves very quickly, and the process does not seem to hurt or cause them any distress. When they are in werewolf form they become telepathic, being able to read the minds of the members in their pack. Although they are strong and short-tempered, they are protectors of La Push, and they often trawl the woods in their pack, hunting for predatory vampires. Jacob is everything that a werewolf is not supposed to be: caring, controlled and sensitive. He does not infect and transform others, uncontrollably killing and howling at the full moon. Jacob abandons the classic stereotype and is the evolved modernized version. A central theme to the *Twilight* series is vampires vs werewolves. This has been reflected in the promotion of the series, as the actors playing Edward and Jacob, Robert Pattinson and Taylor Lautner, have been pitted against each other in a war over who has the biggest fanbase.

Scene still from *The Twilight Saga: New Moon*, Chris Weitz, 2009.

OTHER WEREWOLF FILMS

THE WEREWOLF
(1913)

The first werewolf film. A Navajo Witch Woman transforms her daughter into a wolf in order to attack the invading white men. An actual wolf was used in the transformation sequence. Directed by Henry Macrae, it is a silent short film, considered to be a lost masterpiece as it was destroyed in a fire in 1924.

LE LOUP-GAROU
(1923)

An early silent werewolf movie, produced in France by Pierre Bressol and Jacques Roullet and starring Jean Marau and Madeleine Guitty. A murderer is cursed to be a werewolf by a priest.

WEREWOLF OF LONDON
(1935)

Starring Henry Hull and Warner Oland. During his search for a rare Tibetan flower, a respected botanist is forced to defend himself from a howling monster. Back in London he is told the flower is the only antidote for keeping werewolves from harming the ones they love. He is skeptical but at the next full moon, he begins to change his mind. The first movie in which the character changes not into a wolf, but a mixture of man and wolf.

THE UNDYING MONSTER
(1942)

A film version of Jessie Douglas Kerruish's 1922 novel. The Hammonds are cursed with lycanthropy, something that is found out after Howard goes on a tirade through the town. He is eventually shot by the police.

HOUSE OF DRACULA
(1945)

Lon Chaney Jnr gives *The Wolf Man* Larry Talbot a third airing. Talbot is finally cured by a mad doctor but his attempt to also cure Dracula backfires and he turns himself into a vampire. Frankenstein's monster is revived and the film builds to the customary cataclysmic climax. Talbot finally walks away cured, and the trilogy ends happily ever after.

THE WEREWOLF
(1956)

A man is found unconscious in a car crash by two scientists. They take him back as a guinea pig to their lab and inject him with a serum they have been developing. Unfortunately, he turns into a psychokiller werewolf...

Film poster for *The Werewolf*, Fred F. Sears, 1956.

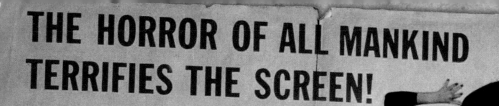

THE HORROR OF ALL MANKIND TERRIFIES THE SCREEN!

SCIENTISTS TURN MEN INTO BEASTS!

YOU SEE IT HAPPEN!

THE WEREWOLF

with

DON MEGOWAN · **JOYCE HOLDEN**

introducing **STEVEN RITCH** as **THE WEREWOLF**

Story and Screen Play by ROBERT E. KENT and JAMES B. GORDON
Produced by SAM KATZMAN · Directed by FRED F. SEARS
A CLOVER PRODUCTION · A COLUMBIA Picture

THE CURSE OF THE WEREWOLF
(1961)

This adaptation of Guy Ender's novel *The Werewolf of Paris* features Leon, played by Oliver Reed who is born on Christmas Eve, son of a mute servant girl who has been raped by a beggar. A patch of hair on his arm, along with his Christmas Eve birth signifies lycanthropy, but he has a quiet life until a brush with a prostitute unleashes his other self.

THE COMPANY OF WOLVES
(1979)

A Gothic fantasy-horror film, starring Angela Lansbury and Sarah Patterson and directed by Neil Jordan, based on the werewolf story of the same name by English novelist, Angela Carter. It is a Freudian and vaguely feminist re-telling of the tale *Little Red Riding Hood*. Lansbury plays Grandma who tells her dreaming granddaughter (Patterson) bizarre stories of handsome yet heavily eye-browed strange men, spouses who disappear during full moons, and storks and eggs.

THE HOWLING
(1981)

Director Joe Dante's film features a news anchor, Karen (Dee Wallace) who is used as a decoy to catch a psychopath who has a past tainted with lycanthropy. She ends up at The Colony, a remote countryside resort populated by a pack of werewolves. Karen burns The Colony and its occupants and makes her escape, but during her first newscast following her return, she transforms into a werewolf.

WOLF
(1994)

Will Randall, played by Jack Nicholson, is bitten by a wolf while driving late at night and becomes a werewolf. From that point on, his life changes as he uses his newly acquired wolf instincts to gain advantages over his colleagues and take revenge on his enemies.

GINGER SNAPS
(2000)

Ginger Snaps tells the story of two teenage sisters, Ginger and Brigitte Fitzgerald (Katharine Isabelle and Emily Perkins), who are obsessed with death. On the night of Ginger's first period, she is savagely attacked by a wild creature. Her wounds heal miraculously but something is not quite right. Now Brigitte must save her sister and herself. Critics praised the performances of lead actresses, Katharine Isabelle and Emily Perkins, and the film's clever use of lycanthropy as a metaphor for puberty.

WILD COUNTRY
(2006)

A group of Glasgow teenagers on a hike through the Scottish Highlands discover an abandoned baby in the ruins of a castle. As they attempt to get the baby to safety a mysterious wolf-like beast suddenly appears in the darkness and begins stalking them, intent on killing them one by one. They soon realize they must kill the beast before it slaughters every one of them.

Scene still from *Howling VI*, Hope Perello, 1991.

THE LYCANTHROPE
(2007)

Three friends are on a road trip to the home of one friend's deceased relative to gather personal belongings and documents. Locals in the town are puzzled by several bizarre murders that have taken place recently. The friends settle in for a night at the house but one of them runs into something unexplainable and unexpected while venturing out into the grounds around the house.

WAR WOLVES
(2009)

A group of US soldiers return from a tour of duty in the Middle East to find that they can grow fangs at will and transform themselves. Horrified by their growing taste for blood, they part. Refusing to give in, one finds a life away from it all, going under the name of Lawrence Talbot, in a reference to Lon Chaney Jnr's character. However, he learns that it is impossible to escape from the werewolf life as members of his pack try to hunt him down and convert him to the thrills of their new lupine existence.

UNDERWORLD:
RISE OF THE LYCANS
(2009)

A prequel to the Underworld series of films, this movie traces the origins of the centuries-old blood feud between the aristocratic vampires known as Death Dealers and their onetime slaves, the Lycans.

Scene still from the *Underworld* series.

WEREWOLVES ON TELEVISION

DARK SHADOWS
(1966—71)

A hugely popular gothic soap opera, which followed the bizarre lives of the Collins family and their friends. The show featured werewolves, ghosts, zombies, man-made monsters, witches, warlocks and time travel. Now regarded as something of a camp classic, it is remembered for its melodramatic performances, atmospheric interiors, memorable storylines, and an adventurous music score. Johnny Depp is currently collaborating with director Tim Burton on a film adaptation.

THE DRAK PACK
(1980—82)

In this animated series, Count Dracula's great-nephew leads a team of superheroes made up of his friends in an effort to make up for the havoc created by his uncle. They transform into teenage versions of Dracula, the Frankenstein Monster and a werewolf and fight against the evil Dr Dred and his minions.

DR WHO: THE GREATEST SHOW IN THE GALAXY
(1988—89)

Werewolves feature in a couple of series of the long running BBC sci-fi hit, *Dr. Who*. In *The Greatest Show in the Galaxy*, the evil Captain Cook attempts to turn the Doctor's assistant, Mags, into a werewolf.

SHE-WOLF OF LONDON
(1990—91)

In this short-run series, a female American student in London is bitten by a werewolf, then teams up with an English professor. The pair investigate supernatural occurrences while he searches for a cure for her.

BUFFY THE VAMPIRE SLAYER
(1997—2003)

The American television series *Buffy the Vampire Slayer* has come to be regarded as a classic. It brought a host of frightening supernatural characters to television in a show aimed at teenagers, and best of all: they were being defeated by a teenage girl! The creator, Josh Whedon, saw a gap in entertainment for a powerful female lead character who, as well as being attractive, would be strong and interesting, appealing to both genders. While Buffy is busy slaying vampires, it is her friend Oz, who becomes a werewolf.

One night, a beautiful full moon is glowing in Sunnydale. Cordelia and Xander are in a car when suddenly a creature rips a hole in the car's roof. We later learn that there have been some other mysterious incidents around this time; animals being killed, students being bitten, and Oz has reported being bitten by a cousin. Giles, Buffy's father figure and mentor, explains that werewolves maintain their form for three nights when

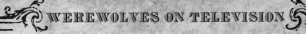

the moon is at its fullest, and that the following night would be the second of the three. As a werewolf is human for the other days of the month, Giles claims it would be wrong to kill one, concluding that werewolves are attracted by 'sexual heat', and that teenagers will be likely targets. The next day, Oz wakes up in a forest, naked and confused. He thinks back to his cousin biting him, and starts to wonder if there is a connection between that, and his situation. He phones his Aunt and asks her outright if his cousin is a werewolf; bizarrely, she confirms his fears and he realizes he has been infected with the curse. Meanwhile Willow, Oz's girlfriend, has become increasingly frustrated by Oz's lack of commitment to her, and all the mixed messages he has been sending her, and on Buffy's advice she goes to see Oz, just as the sun is about to set. She does not know, but Oz is at his house, preparing to chain himself up in order to control the beast he turns into. He is interrupted by Willow knocking at the door, and despite the bad timing, lets her in. She begins to tell him how she feels when suddenly he starts to change. Terrified, Willow screams and flees the house, with Oz hot on her trail. Buffy and Giles have since figured all of this out, and load a tranquilizer gun meant for Oz. They all end up in a clearing in the forest and Willow ends up being the one who shoots Oz, saving everyone from him and his deadly bite. Much later in the series, Oz travels to Tibet to learn techniques that will help him control his condition. When he comes back from his trip, he is no longer at the mercy of a full moon. Negative emotions, however, such as pain or anger, can still trigger a transformation, so although he has his inner wolf under control, it still lives within him, constantly threatening to break free.

The cast of US TV series *Buffy the Vampire Slayer*, which aired between 1997 and 2003.

CHARMED
(1998–2006)

An American series that follows the four Halliwell sisters - Prue, Piper, Phoebe and, later, Paige. They are the culmination of the most powerful line of good witches in history. The sisters, despite being perceived as normal women by the non-supernatural community, are known as The Charmed Ones in the magical community, with the destiny of protecting against evil beings, such as demons and warlocks. A werewolf-like creature known as a Wendigo (see page 90) appears.

BIG WOLF ON CAMPUS
(1999–2002)

A lighthearted Canadian teen series about a boy named Tommy Dawkins who is bitten by a werewolf the week before he returns to school for his senior year. Now a werewolf himself, he battles against vampires, cat women, ghosts, zombies and other supernatural beings to keep his home town Pleasantville safe, even though the entire town thinks the 'Pleasantville Werewolf' is dangerous.

BEN 10
(2005–2008)

An animated series about a boy who has an alien device attached to his arm that allows him to turn into alien creatures. Werewolves feature in several episodes.

DR WHO: TOOTH AND CLAW
(2006)

The Doctor and Rose are transported to 19th-century Scotland, where they meet Queen Victoria, and try to protect her from a ravenous werewolf and a band of murderous warrior-monks. Prince Albert informs the Doctor that the werewolf is really the current form of an alien species that fell to Earth in 1540 near the monastery, surviving by passing its lycanthropic form from human to human.

KAMEN RIDER KIVA
(2008)

In this Japanese series, Wataru Kurenai lives in a notorious haunted house where as the superhero, Kamen Rider Kiva, he fights the life-sapping monsters, the Fangires, monsters with whom his father had fought before his mysterious disappearance 22 years previously. Monsters such as werewolves, vampires and Frankenstein's monster make appearances.

BEING HUMAN
(2008–)

BBC comedy-drama series *Being Human* is about two twenty-somethings living in Bristol. George, who happens to be a werewolf and Mitchell, who is a vampire, move into a flatshare only to discover that their new home is haunted by Annie, the ghost of a previous tenant. They each struggle with their afflictions, and George goes to extreme lengths to try and control the wolf inside him. Every month, when the moon is at its fullest, George begins to transform.

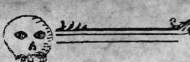

He usually knows when this will happen, and so takes himself off somewhere remote, sometimes stripping naked so as not to rip his clothes when his body shape changes. When he starts to 'phase', his spine becomes bent and awkward, his fingernails grow and fangs replace his teeth. Hair grows all over his body and head, and within seconds there is nothing of the human left. The vampire Mitchell describes the condition that plagues his flatmate:

He should be dead within 30 seconds. The werewolf heart is about two-thirds the size of a human's. But in order to shrink, first it has to stop. In other words, he has a heart attack. All of the internal organs are smaller, so while he's having his heart attack, he's having liver and kidney failure too. If he stops screaming it's not because the pain has dulled, his throat, gullet and vocal chords are tearing and reforming. He literally can't make a sound. By now the pituitary gland should be working overtime, flooding his body with endorphins to ease some of the pain, but that too has shut down. Anyone else would have died of shock long ago. But it won't kill him and that's the thing I find most remarkable. It drags him through the fire and keeps him alive and even conscious to endure every second. Nothing like this could just evolve. This... is the fingerprint of God. An impossible lethal curse spread by tooth and claw, victim begets victim begets victim. It's so cruel, it's... perfect.

In werewolf form, George is the exact opposite of the mild-mannered geeky character he is in the daytime. George is often repulsed by his affliction, referring to it merely as something that happens to him once a month, and naming the wolf 'it', rather than admitting it to be an extension of himself. When he first became a werewolf

he moved away from his fiancee, family and job as he knew he would never be able to live a normal life, and that he was a danger to those he loved the most. As the series progresses, we see George try and literally contain the problem, by placing himself in a cage, downing tranquilizers, and allowing Annie, his ghost flatmate, to keep him locked up. Of course, this did not have the desired effect, as it just angers his inner wolf, and causes him to become bad-tempered throughout the rest of the month.

DEMONS
(2009)

This British drama series about the supernatural follows the adventures of London teenager, Luke Rutherford, who learns that he is the last descendant of the Van Helsing family line, Professor Abraham Van Helsing being the famous vampire hunter of Bram Stoker's 1897 novel, *Dracula*. His uncle arrives from America to tell him this and to teach him about 'half-lives' - vampires, werewolves, zombies and demons.

TRUE BLOOD
(2008-)

Bon Temps is a small town in Louisiana with some very interesting residents. Sookie Stackhouse, the central character, is a waitress with a strange and special ability: she is telepathic. She's unusual in the romance department too, having fallen in love with local vampire Bill Compton. Sookie learns to control her telepathy, concentrating hard to tune out the voices she hears constantly. When she meets Bill for the first time, she is delighted to discover that she can't hear his thoughts at all. The reasons for Sookie's telepathy are unclear at this time, and she is viewed with suspicion by some members of the community. Most of the action takes place in Merlotte's, the main meeting point for Bon Temp's residents and the bar where Sookie works. Sam, the owner, is in love with Sookie, and feels protective towards her. In season one we discover that the dog often seen at Sookie's side is actually Sam, who reveals himself as a shapeshifter. In Merlotte's we learn that many of the patrons are not impressed that Sookie is dating a vampire, as there are a lot of people that do not agree vampires should mix with mortals. There is a constant struggle between the people that accept vampires as ordinary citizens, and those that do not. Those that accept them are considered to be 'fang bangers', and looked on with disgust, and those that do not accept them are seen as bigoted. Of course, it would be foolish to cross a vampire, as mortals are no match for a vampire's otherworldly strength, but some of the ignorant locals do so anyway. As the first season progresses, we learn about other vampires living in and around Bon Temps, some good natured and some not. As Sookie ventures deeper and deeper into the vampire underworld, she finds herself delving into the rules of the supernatural and, due to her telepathy, becomes a person of special interest to the vampire authorities. By season two, other supernatural characters start to appear. A heart-eating maenad (a mystical creature from Greek mythology) arrives and turns all of Bon Temps into mindless servants with her magical powers. By season three, werewolves make their debut in the form of Alcide Herveaux, Debbie Pelt, Coot and Gus. The werewolves in *True Blood* work for the vampire king of Mississippi, Russell Edgington. Alcide is a 'good werewolf', and much like many of the male characters in *True Blood*, he becomes attracted to Sookie. Traditionally in fiction there is a vampire vs werewolves theme, but here Russell is in charge of the pack and has had werewolves in his service for centuries, providing them with blood to satisfy their appetites. As the season goes on we learn the complex relationships within the wolf pack, and why vampire Eric has such a deep hatred for his werewolf associates. HBO used real wolves to film their werewolf scenes, and their promotional poster featured the head of a wolf with glowing orange eyes, and one word: bewere.

Scene still showing Joe Manganiello as werewolf Alcide Herveaux in US TV series *True Blood*, 2008-present.

POPULAR MUSIC

Teenagers have long identified with the monster genre and in particular the outsider nature of the werewolf, the loner who does not fit into today's society. This has been reflected in a wide range of popular songs that transcend the genres from rock to folk and from ballad to heavy metal.

WHITE MOUNTAIN
Genesis

Recorded for the 1970 album *Trespass*, by Genesis, a song about Fang 'son of Great Fang', who may or may not be a werewolf. Arrant nonsense.

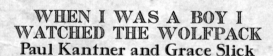

WHEN I WAS A BOY I WATCHED THE WOLFPACK
Paul Kantner and Grace Slick

'Laser bright feel the lunar light comin' down on me/Moonlight, leave me be, comin' down on me'. Paul Kantner and Grace Slick of the great San Francisco psychedelic rock band, Jefferson Airplane, probably over-indulged before coming up with this tale of a werewolf for their 1971 album *Sunfighter*.

WEREWOLVES OF LONDON
Warren Zevon

From the mordantly humorous Warren Zevon's 1978 album *Excitable Boy*, this song is memorable for Zevon's customarily macabre lyrics with lines such as 'I saw a werewolf drinking a piña colada at Trader Vic's, his hair was perfect!' It reached number 21 on the American charts, the only time the late singer had a solo hit record.

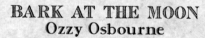

BARK AT THE MOON
Ozzy Osbourne

You get the feeling that Ozzy might have personal experience of this. He sings about the eerie sounds after the monster rises from the grave to take revenge.

I WAS A TEENAGE WEREWOLF
The Cramps

The American garage punk band featured this song on their first album 1980's *Songs the Lord Taught Me*. The opening verse goes: 'I was a teenage werewolf/Braces on my fangs/I was a teenage werewolf/And no one even said thanks/And no one made me stop'.

Photograph of Ozzy Osbourne dressed as werewolf for the *Bark At The Moon* album cover shoot.

THRILLER
Michael Jackson

Michael Jackson's 1983 hit *Thriller* is probably one of the most iconic music videos of all time. It lasts an impressive 14 minutes and tells the story of a young man on a date with his girlfriend, and then revealing to her his secret: he is a werewolf. He then, as clouds pass and reveal the full moon, begins to convulse and strain. Suddenly, he bends down, his girlfriend asks, 'are you alright?', and a second later he's back in the shot, but this time with yellow glowing eyes and a mouth full of fangs. As his girlfriend stands screaming, his eyes start to bulge, his face changes shape, his ears become pointed and his skin seems to shrivel and ooze. Pointed, thick nails tear through his fingertips and long whiskers shoot out from around his mouth. Throughout his transformation his screams turn to growls and eventually he lets out a terrifying roar, as his girlfriend flees the scene. He tears through the woods searching for her, stopping occasionally to howl into the night. As she runs he jumps out at her, scaring her to the ground. He stands over her, lowering his claws to dig into her, when suddenly the scene switches to a cinema, and a couple are watching the werewolf movie on the big screen. The audience scream at the film, and Michael Jackson smiles widely at it, eating popcorn while everyone around him is visibly shocked. Michael's girlfriend is very scared and storms out, he then follows her as the familiar beat of *Thriller* starts. The couple walk through the town and past a graveyard as zombies force their way out of their graves, finally cornering the pair in a street. When she turns to Michael she sees he has become a zombie too, and after the infamous dance routine, she runs away and hides in an abandoned house, where the zombies quickly find her and break in. As she cowers the zombies approach her, Michael places a hand on her and she screams - a second later they are gone and Michael is back to normal, laughing at her for behaving so strangely. As the couple walk away in an embrace, Michael turns to the camera with his yellow glowing werewolf eyes, and evil laughter can be heard.

The make-up and special effects may seem rather 'cheesy' to a modern, desensitized audience. But at the time, Rick Baker, who had received an academy award for his make-up work on werewolf classic *An American Werewolf in London* two years previously, did an outstanding job. *Thriller* won many awards and is a staple track at any Halloween party. Before the video starts, a message from Michael is displayed, illustrating fears of being associated with the dark side:

> Due to my strong personal convictions, I wish to stress that this film in no way endorses a belief in the occult.

OF WOLF AND MAN
Metallica

A song from the heavy metal band's 1991 *Metallica* album that is sung by a werewolf. 'Shape shift!' go the backing vocals while the lead vocal sings about his hair standing on the back of his neck. 'So seek the wolf in thyself', he implores at one point.

WEREWOLF
Michael Hurley / Cat Power

American singer-songwriter Michael Hurley's song *Werewolf* is an atmospheric evocation of the anguish of being a werewolf. 'Have sympathy/Because the werewolf he is someone/Just like you and me'. Cat Power's breathless version takes it to an entirely different and scary level.

SHE WOLF
Shakira

The 2010 video for *She Wolf* starts with classic werewolf imagery: a full moon. Shakira opens her eyes and sees the moon, it seems to pull her closer, as if she were under a spell. She looks at her hands and her fingernails grow and become more pointed. She gets out of bed, leaving her lover behind, puts on some boots and enters a walk-in wardrobe. The song then begins and the video is split between her dancing in a sort of cave, which she has stepped into from the wardrobe, and in a cage and on a dancefloor in a club. She dances in an animalistic way, soon joined by back-up dancers in a club, as a wolf stalks the perimeter before turning into a woman. She continues to writhe maniacally in the cage as howling can be heard and her dancing becomes more frantic. Soon, she's dancing on a roof in the glare of the full moon and as the song winds down, she's suddenly back in her walk-in wardrobe. She tiptoes into her bedroom, before looking up at the moon and smiling. Shakira, as a 'she wolf', was able to come alive at night, due to the moon triggering her to change. Her dancing inside the cage represents the wolf inside her, with the actual bars of the cage being the boundaries on her life. The wolf she turns into represents her innermost desires, and how repressed she feels during the day is gladly relieved at night, when the moon is at its fullest. She sings:

A domesticated girl that's
all you ask of me,

Darling it is no joke, this is lycanthropy,

The moon's awake now
with eyes wide open,

My body's craving, so feed the hungry.

It is more frequently suggested in narrative that only men become werewolves, perhaps it is more believable that they have a beast inside them; but here Shakira demonstrates otherwise.

OTHER WEREWOLF-INSPIRED SONGS

Animal - Pearl Jam
Bad Moon Rising - Creedence Clearwater Revival
Cat People (Putting Out Fire) - David Bowie
Cry Wolf - A-Ha
Dire Wolf - Grateful Dead
Full Moon - Robert Miles
Howl - Florence and the Machine
Hungry Like A Wolf - Duran Duran
Juju Nightshift - Siouxsie & the Banshees
Loup Garou Bal Goula - Willy DeVille
Night Wolf - Krokus
Run With The Wolf - Rainbow
The Wolf That Lives In Lindsey - Joni Mitchell
Will the Wolf Survive? - Los Lobos
Witch Wolf - Styx
Wolf of the Moon - Ritchie Blackmore

Scene still from Michael Jackson's *Thriller* music video.
Directed by John Landis, 1983.

INDEX

PICTURE CREDITS

Scene still from *An American Werewolf in Paris*,
Anthony Waller, 1997.

This edition published in 2011 by
CHARTWELL BOOKS, INC.
A division of BOOK SALES, INC.
276 Fifth Avenue Suite 206
New York, New York 10001
USA

© 2011 Omnipress Limited
www.omnipress.co.uk

ISBN-13: 978-0-7858-2729-0
ISBN-10: 0-7858-2729-3

Canary Press
An imprint of Omnipress Ltd
Chantry House, 22 Upperton Road
Eastbourne, East Sussex BN21 1BF
England

Printed in China.